The Last Shot

by

Brett Wallach

Phil Allman, P.I., Book 9

The Last Shot

Cover Art by *Jennifer Greeff*

The Wild Rose Press, Inc.
PO Box 708
Adams Basin, NY 14410-0708
Visit us at www.thewildrosepress.com

Publishing History
First Edition, 2023
Trade Paperback ISBN 978-1-5092-4867-4
Digital ISBN 978-1-5092-4868-1

Phil Allman, P.I., Book 9
Published in the United States of America

I have a particular aversion to men who strike women. I didn't want to schlep all the way to Manhattan to have a go with Rachel's ex Kret, but if she and I grew closer, I knew that I may have to. Other than losing a marriage or two, it didn't seem like he paid much of a price for his brutality and philandering, and I'm a believer in paying for your sins, especially those that hurt others. I'm a middle-aged semi-retired schnook, after all, but I was a semi-retired schnook who still had the ability and desire to beat the shit out of most asshole men. I'd have Dan give me more intelligence about Kret should I decide to visit him; if he was a secret black belt or something, I was also too old a schnook to get the shit beat out of me.

Meanwhile, I figured I'd write a new novel. About what exactly? How's a book about a semi-retired Private Investigator writing a novel and using, one way or the other, an old high school acquaintance, who's now a big muckety-muck in the publishing industry, to get a book deal sound?

Dedication

To Valerie and Alison as always.
Thanks to the great editor, Lea Schizas, and everyone at
TWRP for their unfettered help and support.

Part One

Chapter 1

Sometimes, I drive recklessly through the pockmarked streets and avenues of my Northeast Philadelphia neighborhood. I'm in no hurry to get anywhere; I have no particular place to go, to quote Chuck Berry. I secretly hope that someone will crash into me. Or that I'll crash into someone. I have no death wish and I don't get off on pain.

I just crave the human contact. Even if I might get hurt.

I was in that headspace when I saw Rachel Arison's profile on Facebook.

****

It is the beginning of the fourth quarter for me, actuarially. Time is running out, I'm way behind, and I've got to score. Now. I don't have time to dink and dunk; I need a long Hail Mary pass to the end zone. The question is: Do I still have the strength to chuck the ball downfield?

Thoughts of getting older resonate, especially when I access social media. Everybody's happy and everybody's getting laid. Open any of the popular social media apps. Your prospective romantic partner or kid you knew back in middle school is always having the best time ever and seemingly always fucking, and if you want to get on that train, it's supposedly never been easier to jump on board.

I have no kick against happiness or sex. This is a rough world, baby, and you do what you need to. The dating app girls say they want to fuck away their pain and get all nice and 420-friendly. I hold no ill will toward them. It's just that the omnipresent message of everyone attaining ecstasy all the time is grating after a while. Especially if you're not. Twenty-first century literature, especially the mystery genre, my heretofore go-to get-away from incessant Internet hedonism? No escape there.

The only shades of gray in modern fiction come in blocks of fifty.

When I present my novel queries to the agents and publishers, their no-comment rejections all seem to scream: *Hey, where's all the sex and drugs and happiness?* My books are edgy, violent, and ribald, yes, but *everybody* isn't merrily getting laid *all the time.* For my characters that have to work for it, it's not like picking off the low-hanging apples on a tree; they have to climb at least a little bit for their treat. I've gotten reviews and emails complaining about the sex and bad language in my books, and there's fucking plenty of both, but that's not *all* there is.

I explain all of this to Rachel Arison, yet somehow, she is not empathetic. But I am getting ahead of myself. Let me tell you briefly how we got here. The backstory if you will, even though the writing advice books say to avoid it because people gloss over it.

I graduated from high school. Barely.

I was married twice. Barely.

I am still a licensed, working Private Investigator. Barely.

And I have been a published author. Barely. You see, I was involved in a couple of high-profile cases years ago; I was the detective who found Elvis Presley's twin brother, thought to be stillborn, as documented in *Jesse Garon* (the name of Elvis's real-life twin, search it); and I helped New Jersey rock legend Felix Brigati escape from a kidnapper, as chronicled in *Freeze Out*. I worked with a couple of small publishers that took advantage of my status as a very minor celebrity, and they published these and about a half-dozen of my other P.I. books. Both companies eventually went out of business like so many in the modern-day book world, but I kind of got the hang of writing. I eventually had to go the soul-crushing, cachet-killing self-publishing route after the companies' demise.

There are no delusions in my mind about my writing ability, but I think my stuff is at least as good as most of the crap out there. It's as much whom (note the proper grammar) you know as what you write. I don't attend writers' conferences and symposiums like you're supposed to in order to make connections because I have a job and responsibilities and social anxiety. I'm also not after great fortune and fame, but, you know, a little of each would be nice before I go off to The Big Sleep (the rare mystery novel worthy of its fortune and fame).

My books have also been called vulgar, misogynistic, racist, simplistic, and self-indulgent. And that's by my friends and family. But most objective readers and reviewers have said they're funny, suspenseful, insightful, and even romantic, at times. But once you've been published by the little guys, and worst of all, self-published, agents and publishers simply will not read your stuff. It's like the scarlet letter. But I think I'm good, and I aim to prove it.

Rachel Arison is fifty-five years old, graduated from Penn with a Master's in English, is divorced with no children, and is one of the most powerful people in the world of Publishing as a Senior VP at the renowned publishing house Bryce Douglas. She used to work out of their Park Avenue Manhattan offices until Covid hit, and then she came back to Philly to take care of her father, who unfortunately contracted the virus and subsequently passed away. She stayed and joined much of the rest of the professional world on Zoom and Teams calls and took the train up to Manhattan sporadically for important meetings and whatnot.

She lives in a de-luxe apartment in the sky (old person cultural reference) on Rittenhouse Square, the most expensive and exclusive section of Philadelphia. Though an attractive, fit blonde, Rachel is a loner and a reader; I felt a kinship toward her. She worked out at a posh Center City gym at seven in the morning almost every weekday, mostly ate her meals alone at home, and had few friends and family members to whom she was close, either in Philadelphia or New York.

Rachel grew up in the same Northeast Philadelphia neighborhood (albeit in a better section of it), and graduated from the same high school in the same year as I. Straight A student in all advanced courses, with all the cliched trappings one associates with that kind of kid. Though we shared no classes, we attended the same homeroom all through high school due to alphabetic assignment. While she cites the classics as her favorite literature, Rachel mostly reads sexy, edgy mysteries both for work and for pleasure.

Much of this info was easily gleaned from her official Bryce Douglas bio and Facebook posts which I stumbled upon (Facebook recommended her as a "friend"); Dan Lee, my best friend and independent contractor for all things technological, whom you will meet later, picked up the rest. She was living in my town, reading my kind of books, and had precious little contact with the outside world. I'd say that she was as good a candidate as any.

****

"Rachel? Rachel Arison?"

I hate mornings and have been fortunate not to have to wake up to an alarm for most of my adult life. I had signed up for a free trial workout at her fancy-schmancy gym on Nineteenth and Walnut, got my lazy ass up at five, had a bowl of granola and six cups of coffee for breakfast, got in my car, and made the hour-plus drive (including a pee break) to arrive at Physique at six forty-five. It was early November, before the guilt-ridden started working off their holiday meals, and the gym was sparsely attended at that early hour by people of both genders, wearing outfits that cost more than my monthly utilities. I am a humble man, but I'm pretty ripped for an old guy.

Rachel looked at me and showed faint recognition but couldn't remember my name. That's okay. It was likely that she didn't know it even when we went to high school together almost forty years ago. "Phil. Phil Allman", I said. "We went to Northeast High together."

She nodded, gave me a tense smile, and reached out her hand. "Right. Phil Allman. We had homeroom together, right?" Ya boy leaves a lasting impression after all. "Do you belong here?" Meaning was I a member of Physique, not a question about my socio-economic status for even setting foot in this fancy-schmancy gym and neighborhood. I had stripped down to a tank top and shorts in the locker room, both of which were older than most of the other early morning gym attendees. The place had the same machines as the free gym at my apartment complex in Northeast Philly, but everything, including the two dozen or so men and women there at daybreak, for lack of a better word, *shined*. I felt like I almost had to wear the sunglasses that I used for the hazy drive downtown. It was a Wednesday morning, cold and windy and sunny, and with my old man eyesight, it was difficult driving down I-95 even with my dollar store shades.

"No," I said, prepared for the question. "I'm attending a conference and am staying downtown for a few nights. To be honest, I signed up for a free trial workout. Don't tell anyone," I said, putting my forefinger to my lips indicating mum's the word, sharing a great conspiracy with her.

"My lips are sealed." She was wearing a cute baby blue top and tight black sweats, very little if any makeup, and her bleached blonde hair was tied in a bun. Overall fetching for seven in the morning, but not attention-seeking. "It's nice to see you." She was ready to give me the brush, but smooth talker that I am, I kept at it.

"Do you live in Center City?"

Not wanting to be impolite, she said, "Yes, I recently moved back to the area from Manhattan." I already knew all of this, of course, but acted pleased as punch that the esteemed Rachel Arison returned home.

"That's awesome." Okay, maybe smooth talker was an overstatement. "Listen, I don't mean anything by this, but might you want to get a drink later? Maybe dinner? I don't know anyone around here, and it sounds like you're a Center City newbie too."

It was easy to see the questions spinning in her pretty, educated head. Do I really want to have dinner with this schmuck? He seems nice and safe enough, not terrible looking (at least that's my interpretation of her unsaid thoughts), and I'm not doing anything later, anyway. Why not? "Why not?" See? "I don't know about dinner, but maybe we can grab a drink. Where are you staying?"

I was prepared for this question too. "The Warwick."

"Okay. How about if I meet you in the lobby at seven this evening? It might be fun to catch up. You're right, I don't know many people in my new neighborhood."

"Sounds good Rachel, see you then." I then proceeded to the universal weight machines, and she meandered to a treadmill. Everything was going according to plan. Easier in fiction than in real life.

****

"So, what do you do, Phil?"

This was Rachel and me, or is it Rachel and I? They have editors at these publishing companies, they can figure it out. After I left the gym at around eight, I drove back home, took a quick shower, and booked a room online at the Warwick for two nights, packing the nicest clothes that I have. Which weren't objectively nice. I brought a grayish twenty-year-old suit, a purple shirt and tie, a couple of other whitish shirts and colorful ties, a plaid-ish sport jacket, a bottle of cologne that I got for Father's Day about ten years ago, and a pair of scuffed black shoes.

After I checked in to my room late that afternoon, I took another quick shower, put on my go-to-meetin' clothes, and dabbed on a little cologne to hopefully drown out my anxiety sweat. Rachel was already in the lobby when I got off the elevator at seven sharp, wearing a conservative navy pantsuit, I think that's what you call it, I don't know, but she looked cute if that isn't an inappropriate word to say about a fifty-five-year-old publishing executive. She suggested that we walk to Curly's, an upscale tavern a block away, and we sat at a back table in the dark, expensive bar.

I felt as fishy as a fish out of water as one could. The place was about half full of wealthy-looking middle-aged white people in a town where us whites are the minority. Nobody there probably thought about that as they drank their martinis and whatever else rich people drank. Rachel ordered a gin and tonic. I was going to get a beer, thought better of it, and ordered the same from the semi-hot young waitress. "This will sound like something from an old movie, but I'm a private investigator," answering her earlier question.

The chemistry between us wasn't romantic or sexual, or even friendly. It was that of two distant acquaintances who hadn't seen each other in decades, which made sense. But she visibly perked up at the announcement of my career. "Ooh, that sounds interesting! Like your namesake Philip Marlowe. You could write a book about it." Yes.

"My life and career really aren't that interesting." But then I just happened to mention the Jesse Garon

Presley and Felix Brigati cases, both of which she well remembered from the extensive media coverage at the time and the fact that I wrote short narratives about each and that they, along with several other of my books, had been published by two different small houses. At this, her pretty ears pricked up again. This was going even better than I had hoped.

"I work in Publishing. But I'm unfamiliar with your books. With whom did you work?" At which point, I had to recount the now defunct companies and their eventual demise, as well as the fact that I now was forced to self-publish at which she visibly winced. "I know that there have been a lot of mergers and changes recently, and the small houses rarely survive. But keep at it, and you never know what can happen. The market is always in need of good writers and good stories, no matter what anyone says."

She was giving me the "don't call us, we'll call you" brush-off, but I didn't exactly expect her to whip out a contract and have me sign it. That would come later. "When I scan the mystery aisles, whether at a bookstore, online, or even at the library, it seems like most of the writing about detectives is formulaic," I said. "Honest but flawed dick does all the right things for all the right reasons, usually on behalf of a woman who's been through the mill until this selfless, tireless investigator comes into her life, usually working pro bono. It's all bullshit, excuse me, but it is."

Rachel nodded and gave me a slight "That's the way it is" shrug. "People like formulas, Phil. They're comforting and marketable."

"And boring and unrealistic." She seemed not to want to have this conversation, so I backed off. "I'm sorry. You must hear this kind of complaint from fledgling, unpublished writers all the time. Let's talk about other things." And so, we did.

****

For those of you waiting for details of the assignation, I am sorry to report that it did not occur. I won't lie. I was staying at a nice hotel with a king-size bed, and the thought crossed my mind. I knew from Dan Lee's deeper dive into her background that Rachel was straight and unattached, but our drink did not produce that kind of chemistry. I was a bit nervous, and she was more than a bit wary, and that mix doesn't result in Love Potion #9. But we ended the hour-long session on a good note, exchanged numbers, and I would even say as friends, which was a good start. I didn't expect to fuck my way into a publishing deal anyway and knew Rachel had too much integrity for that, even if I had been Brad Pitt with Shaquille O'Neal's dick. The idea was for her to feel comfortable with me, let her guard down, and then I'd do what I had to.

Because time was running out. No more football metaphors. But if I was going to leave my mark on the world, and attain just a touch of immortality, it had to come from Rachel Arison. If I felt like I was a cheat, just a hack with nothing to say, I would have felt guilty. But I felt worthy of a major publishing deal, and it was only my inability to make a connection and get a foot in the door that had prevented me from scoring one.

I texted Dan to run a thorough report on the life and times of Rachel Arison. I was going full Groundhog Day on this.

Chapter 2

"Herro Joe, what do you know?" For those of you new to my saga, this was my friend and computer guy Dan Lee on the phone. Dan was Asian-American, yes, but he was born and raised in Philadelphia, had gone to Wharton for his various degrees, and to the best of my knowledge had never stepped foot on the Asian continent. Still, he sometimes spoke in this Charlie Chan dialect because he was more than a little crazy.

"Not now, Dan. Speak the King's English or you don't get paid." Dan was the best at what he did as an IT contractor, and accordingly, he was the most expensive. He, like I, was semi-retired, but he still did business with a few key contacts, and I considered myself fortunate enough to be one of them.

"Right-o. Pip pipcheerio, and God save the Queen."

"That's *too* English. Come on, Dan, I need your help, and I'm paying you a lot of money to get it."

"Okay, sorry, Phil. Beyond the basics that I already gave you, Rachel Arison was born and raised in Northeast Philadelphia, went to Penn as you know, has been with Bryce Douglas for over twenty-five years, moving up the ladder to Senior VP of Fiction, making her among the most influential executives at the firm, and thus, in the publishing industry. She was married for almost twenty years to a Stanley Kret. A ne'er-do-well salesman from New York. No kids. Allegations of mental and physical abuse were part of the divorce settlement, meaning that because Rachel was the primary breadwinner, Kret got not a dime in alimony. They've been divorced for over five years. And you know about her moving back to Philly to take care of the dad and that she simply stayed after he passed."

"Dan, I could have gone to her LinkedIn page to get most of that, Jesus Christ. I need to know her personal tastes and wants, that kind of thing."

"Oh, so more of a dating profile? Is that your game here, Phil?"

"No. But yes, on the more personal side of her nature."

Dan hesitated. He knew I was capable of, shall we say, malfeasance, and while he had been an accessory in the past, he always was so grudgingly. "Where is this going, Phil?"

"Into your bank account, Dan, unless you don't provide the information for which I am paying you rather handsomely."

Another hesitation. "This Kret guy was not a good husband. Almost certainly abused her, almost certainly cheated on her. He actually remarried four years ago and divorced in the past two. The new wife, younger of course, also claimed cruelty. Rachel is a loner for sure. No close friends or family left in Philly, a few work-related acquaintances up in Manhattan. She's done the dating app thing as we all have, but she rarely goes out. Obviously, she gets free books from Bryce Douglas, but she frequents Amazon and her Center City library for books quite frequently. Almost all fiction. Mostly crime fiction. Many of the same writers that you tend to like,

Phil. James M. Cain, Walter Mosley, Elmore Leonard, Chandler and Hammett, etc. She worked directly with novelists in the past, but in her senior executive position, she is in more of a management and advisory role, though when she champions an author, she really moves the needle for him or her. Usually him."

All of this was interesting and helpful, but I needed more. "All of this is interesting and helpful, Dan, but I need more." See? Sorry, I won't do that again. "Any, well, quirks or personality flaws?"

The motherfucker paused on me again. "She, um. Well, maybe because of her failed marriage to Kret, she has a touch of a kinky side. She's not on Fetlife or anything, and it's subtle, but in checking her emails and texts to suitors over the past few years, she can be a bit dominant."

I audibly swallowed. "Manifesting itself how?"

"I really don't know. She is reticent to put things in writing, as expected of someone in her position. She tends to be very cautious and suspicious. Almost to the point of paranoia. But she has intimated that she likes to be "Mommy" to a couple of guys. I didn't take any Psych classes at Wharton, but maybe that goes back to her being dominated by Kret and not having children. I only surmise that because there is nothing else in the first fifty years of her life, or certainly in the last couple of decades since the Internet, which showed that aspect of her personality. Does that help?"

I did not answer. "How about movies, music, other interests?"

"She likes the standard movie classics, with a bent toward noir as you would figure. Big Bogart fan. Likes all kinds of music, but being of our generation, she has a leaning toward classic rock, but also veers off to classical and jazz at times, according to her various online purchases and listening habits."

"What else?"

"She's rich. Not as rich as me, but way richer than you. Mid-seven figures socked away in savings and investments. No heirs, but she has a few causes and charities that stand to get much of that money when she passes. Typical Manhattanite liberal stuff. Bleeding heart and all that." I was digesting all of this, and Dan did not speak for what seemed like a month but was probably only twenty seconds. "What are you going to do with all this Phil? She's not a paying client, right? She's divorced from Kret, so she's not paying you for dirt on him. So, what's your game?"

"Dan, I pay you for information. That's all you need to know."

"I'm also your friend. What's going on?"

"Nothing, Marvin Gaye. She's someone that I went to school with, as you know. I recently ran into her, and she's interesting."

"Phil, you're paying me a small fortune for all this. This is more than a passing interest."

"Never mind, Charlie Chan. I'm the detective here. Stay in your lane."

"Oh, solly, so solly, Mister Joe!"

I hung up. I didn't want to deal with his multiple personalities or his digging into my affairs. Like any intelligence, it was up to me now to use the data accumulated to my advantage.

****

Rachel had given me her number over drinks, which was a good sign. I texted her the next morning, suggesting that we meet for lunch or dinner, but she demurred, claiming too much work, whether true or false. I didn't expect "dates" or whatever this was on consecutive days. I asked the Warwick to let me check out early, and happily, the kind folks at the hotel agreed, so I just drove home.

I have a particular aversion to men who strike women. I didn't want to schlep all the way to Manhattan to have a go with Rachel's ex Kret, but if she and I grew closer, I knew that I may have to. Other than losing a marriage or two, it didn't seem like he paid much of a price for his brutality and philandering, and I'm a believer in paying for your sins, especially those that hurt others. I'm a middle-aged semi-retired schnook, after all, but I was a semi-retired schnook who still had the ability and desire to beat the shit out of most asshole men. I'd have Dan give me more intelligence about Kret should I decide to visit him; if he was a secret black belt or something, I was also too old a schnook to get the shit beat out of me.

Meanwhile, I figured I'd write a new novel. About what exactly? How's a book about a semi-retired Private Investigator writing a novel and using, one way or the other, an old high school acquaintance, who's now a big muckety-muck in the publishing industry, to get a book deal sound?

****

Rachel Arison was being polite. We all know the feeling and have likely been on both sides of it. You run into someone you sort of know and you act interested out of politeness when you don't really give a fuck. We don't want that other person to think ill of us or worse, to spread shit about us in our little social circles.

Rachel was my better. It didn't have to be said out loud, I didn't need to see her seven-figure bank statement to confirm it. She was an Ivy League grad living in the swankest part of town, and I was a ham and egger living ghetto adjacent. She had worn her expensive clothes comfortably, and I'd sported my best but still shabby suit like a ten-year-old going to a relative's wedding. I could not expect a woman like Rachel, who worked with some of the most brilliant people on the face of the earth, including the very cream of fiction writers, to take someone like me seriously as a novelist. It was not her fault. She didn't strike me as a snob. But when you've spent twenty-five years at cocktail parties and office receptions mingling with the best and brightest, how seriously could she take someone like me? As either an author or as a romantic suitor? I was a nice diversion for an hour over drinks. Rachel wouldn't use the phrase because she was too polite, but she was slumming it by meeting with me.

It was a matter of perception. She could not overcome her view of me as some insignificant kid who'd graduated in the bottom half of the same high school class where she was in the top one percentile.

I knew what I had to do to get a major publishing deal. Opportunity was knocking. And time was growing short. Was I going to answer the door?

I knew Rachel Arison's schedule. The time had come to act.

****

I hate waking up early. But that following Monday, the weather called for a one hundred percent chance of rain. These weather apps usually hedge their bets, and rarely keep it a hundred, so I felt confident that I wasn't losing a few hours of precious sleep in vain.

Physique was a three-block walk from Rachel's apartment, so the opportunity was perfect. And there she was, wearing a cute light blue raincoat, and carrying a WHYY (Philly's public television station to the uninitiated) umbrella when I pulled up in my Chevy Cruise and gave her a mid-sized honk as she speed-walked west on Walnut. She glanced at me, took a couple of seconds to register who I was, and looked at me quizzically.

I rolled down my window about a quarter of the way. "Rachel, hi. It's Phil Allman. Get in." It wasn't teeming, but it was coming down hard enough that she didn't really question it and hopped around the front of my car to get in my passenger seat.

"Thanks, Phil. Why are you downtown?" We were approaching the busy Seventeenth Street intersection, so this was not the ideal time or place.

"I have a client downtown. I'm glad I saw you or you might have drowned out there."

She laughed. "Well, I hardly think that this is a life-or-death situation, but I appreciate the lift. I'm going to Physique on Nineteenth." I wasn't going to say that I knew, so I just nodded like any good cabbie would. When we got to Eighteenth, I made a sharp left, and pulled up behind a double-parked moving truck. "Phil, why did you turn here?" She did not look at me with alarm—probably figured I misunderstood her destination. At which point, I reached under my car seat, whipped out the white cloth that I had slathered with chloroform, and placed it firmly on Rachel's pretty mouth and nose. She would be out long enough to drive her to my dead uncle's desolate cabin out near Lebanon, Pennsylvania.

Chapter 3

Uncle Jon had surprisingly left me the place in his will. It was a small shack out in the middle of nowhere, an hour and a half west of the city with no neighbors within shouting distance. It was mostly unfurnished, but I paid the small utility bills each month to keep the electricity and water on. It wasn't very cold out, but when we got inside, I turned the thermostat up to sixty-eight and heard the HVAC unit sputter into duty. Rachel couldn't have weighed more than a buck twenty, and she was easy to carry into the house.

She was still unconscious, but I knew from experience that she would be waking up soon, probably in about an hour. Nobody knew or cared where I was. I imagined that since it was nearing nine o'clock, Rachel's firm would expect to hear from her at some point, but she was a high-level executive, so nobody would question her too pointedly about her whereabouts. Unless she had some kind of important virtual meeting that morning, but it was a calculated risk.

To those of you clucking your tongues at me in reproach, I don't blame you. I was not under any circumstances going to hurt Rachel Arison. But I could not let her know that or else all of this was for naught.

I gently laid her (get your mind out of the gutter) on the old green sofa in the living room. I had already stocked the fridge and kitchen cabinets with basic necessities over the previous weekend, as well as the bathroom with essentials. It wasn't a luxury suite at the Warwick, but it was not an uncomfortable place to be held hostage. I'm not a monster.

Those of you who are good at math have already put two and two together, not a difficult puzzle to assemble. I was going to hold Rachel as my, well, *guest* until she greenlighted my next book for a publishing deal with Bryce Douglas. Like I said before, it's whom you know. But because I have a conscience, I would not force this upon her until I felt like I had a worthy manuscript to submit.

Setting the scene is my least favorite part of a book as both a reader and a writer, so I will aim for brevity. Uncle Jon's cabin had hardwood floors throughout, a small living room with the aforementioned sofa, an old three-legged wooden table, a wobbly floor lamp, and an old-fashioned radiator; a tiny bedroom with room only for a single bed and a chest of drawers, upon which sat a dusty desk lamp; a functional small bathroom, a breakfast nook/kitchen with the refrigerator and an old but functional oven; sturdy white walls throughout. No television, no pictures, no frills.

This was a second home for Uncle Jon, for what I don't know, I barely knew the man. Did he come here to get away from the city? Hunt? Fuck? No clue. I couldn't be sure if his leaving it to me was an act of largesse or one of ironic benevolence. Get that tough city boy out of his comfort zone and see how he holds up. Or maybe he wanted someone responsible enough to keep up with the taxes and maintenance. Maybe it was a compliment to my dependability.

Anyway, it was the perfect spot for my purposes. No nosy neighbors. I did not do anything icky with Rachel, but I did take her phone from her raincoat before we started the drive to the country and of course shut it off. I prepared myself for when she woke up. I wanted to appear completely non-threatening, but still scary enough for her to do my bidding. Combination Tom Hanks and Dennis Hopper. I felt guilty watching her rest on the couch. But I had one life to live, one shot at the big time, and this was it.

****

Rachel regained consciousness a little later than I expected, around noon, and not surprisingly, she did a confused once over of the room. Then she saw my face hovering above hers and the confusion continued. She expressed a glimmer of shame, I guess because she thought we hooked up and she couldn't remember it. Not the first woman to have felt like that after waking up next to me. "Phil? Where are we?"

I tried, really tried to be as comforting as one could under these difficult conditions. "Well, Rachel, this is a place that I own out near Lebanon. Pennsylvania, not the Middle East."

"Why are we here?" Confusion turned into anger, and who could blame her?

"Don't freak out. But I have you here because I want Bryce Douglas to publish my next book." At which point, I pulled out an unloaded handgun from the back of my slacks.

Rachel, for all her Manhattan and Ivy League refinement, reacted like a true Philly girl. "Are you out of your fucking mind? Get me the fuck out of here!" I liked this earthy side of her. She could have made a good girlfriend under different circumstances.

"I have a bunch of books already out there. I worked with two different publishers, but they both went out of business, as I told you. Now they're self-published. But I'm good, I swear. I deserve to be published by a company like yours."

"Then submit a fucking query like everybody else. Submit it to me personally, and I promise we'll give it priority. No slush pile."

I expected her to say something like that. "Rachel, we both know that's not how it works. I'm currently a self-published author deep into middle age. My books are good, but they're not immediately audience friendly for a firm like Bryce. I don't have a web presence or a real following. Your being here takes all the guesswork out of it. Bryce Douglas is going to publish my next book. And with it, the rest of my series that's already been in the public domain. Who knows, maybe I'll develop a cult following like a twenty-first-century David Goodis, and you'll be a literary hero for giving me this chance."

Rachel gave me a look that said, you were a high school loser, you're not of my kind, and I'm not going to ruin my well-earned reputation as an advocate for the finest fiction. At least I thought that's what her look said. Maybe she just had to pee. Because she got up, looked around, and went straight for the lavatory, and after exiting it, did not say another word. Not unlike many of my post-marital dates. After her excursion, she sat on the couch like a petulant teenager as if she were alone in the house, and stared at nothing.

"I'm sorry, we don't have cable out here. And I can't allow you to use your phone unsupervised. I thought it might be appropriate for you to read my other books so that you get a handle on my style and give me advice on how to make this next one my best one." I smiled my best smile.

She did not respond. Not unlike many of my post-marital dates. Her reaction was understandable. As angry as Rachel Arison was with me, I had to get her on my side, or at the very least, not have her hate me so much that she would not offer me objective feedback on my writing. I had to use that old Phil Allman charm.

We might be here for a while.

****

I used an app to get dinner delivered, though the place was already stocked with food, as I said. Rachel did not want to contribute her thoughts to other items that she might like, but after I encouraged her and told her that we'd be out here for a good chunk of time, she wrote a list of things that she wanted, and I skimped on none of it. With nothing else to do after our Chinese dinner, she finally acquiesced and read my nine novellas over the next two days, taking copious notes as she went along. I let her use her phone to check for messages and made sure that when she texted or emailed anyone, she said that she had a family emergency and needed a little time away.

And Rachel read my books studiously, using the wobbly floor lamp in the living room. I parked myself in the bedroom as she did so, not wanting to hover or intimidate her further. I wanted objective feedback, and to her credit, that is what she gave me. Abbreviated versions of her reviews are as follows:

"*Jesse Garon*. Overly sentimental, but a nice, marketable idea with some real suspense and humor.

Well executed, I must admit. *And I Love Her*. Not crazy about its disturbing messages, but I love the unexpected ending. *Young Blood.* Very well realized. Funny, and suspenseful. We can do something with this one. I'm surprised that it wasn't more successful. *Freeze Out.* Nice plot twists, but Springsteen's people would sue us in about a minute and a half. *Susceptible.* Very noir, a little too derivative, but good suspense throughout. *Torment.* Good multiracial cast of characters, but again, it's disturbing; more of a cult type of book. *Man Out of Time.* Love the Don Quixote angle and the change of narrator. This is another one that we could work with. *The One You Never Seen Before.* The dual narrators and sexual politics work. To a point." I also gave her the sci-fi/social and political satire novel, *The Last Man On Earth* that I wrote under the pseudonym of Brett Wallach for whatever reason. "First two-thirds are terrific, Phil, very funny and gripping. Then it peters out. But who edited these books? Stevie Wonder?"

I laughed a little. "I basically did it myself."

"It shows. Too many typos and glaring errors for the big leagues. And they're all too short."

"I thought you could combine them, maybe two at a time? Or a couple of anthologies?"

"An anthology for an unknown author? Oh yeah, Bryce will jump up and down with enthusiasm about that. The two at a time could possibly work, though. It's been done. I have to say, Phil, that I am pleasantly surprised. They're not bad. Not all are Bryce Douglas material. But good enough as is for our niche imprints, and a couple of them are ready for the majors right now, with some honing." I felt a flush of pride as she said this while recognizing that she needed to curry favor with me, so I took her praise with a grain of salt.

"Rachel, I want the whole enchilada. I want my novels to be published by Bryce Douglas, not one of your lesser niche brands. And I think I'm the one with the leverage here."

"You don't understand how the publishing industry works. You've worked with a couple of small houses where one person probably ran everything. In the big-time New York publishing world, one person, not even me, can unilaterally greenlight a novel. It has to be approved by a group of people, especially for a new, unknown writer with no built-in audience."

I expected that kind of reaction. "Rachel. If you want to make it out of here, you are somehow going to have to make it happen. You have to decide if you are willing to take a career risk in order to live." I didn't want to sound ominous or dangerous, but I had to go there.

She shook her head like I wasn't grasping what she was saying, a common female reaction to my words. "I'll work on these since I have no other form of entertainment or anything else to do and try to get them up to snuff. I will need access to a laptop with Word. Again, I admit that the germs of good books are there. I just have to allow them to germinate." Good pun.

And to her credit, Rachel Arison, a big time Manhattan publishing executive, did just that over the two days, making numerous revisions on my laptop that I allowed her to use, no Internet access, of course. She helped transform my little gritty books into something better, I must admit. And with that kind of encouragement, I used that time to focus on my next one.

How is it so far?

Chapter 4

"Phil, do your books have to be so violent?" Rachel said, over coffee and breakfast the next morning. "Your protagonist seems to enjoy dishing it out a little too much." I had heard this before, usually from female readers.

"Violence is underrated. When I read mysteries written by most Brits, or to be honest, women, they're lacking good old-fashioned violence. When a man is in a room with another man, or many men, it doesn't matter, he is wondering whose ass he can kick. It's just a dude thing. I don't know—maybe women ask themselves who's prettiest."

"Have you ever been called a Neanderthal, Phil? Trust me, the men whom I know don't think like that at all."

Thinking about the stiff intellectual types that she was probably used to, I believed her. "Well, let's just say most men who aren't part of the upper crust of society think that way. I don't care if they're twenty-five or fifty-five."

"And it's sexist if not misogynistic to say women are always comparing their physical attributes. Maybe generations ago, but not now. And on this, I can speak definitively. I am a woman." She was feeling her oats now, which was cool. I don't like demure women. "One of the reasons that I'm having a hard time editing your books is that there is a strong undercurrent of misogyny throughout them. I don't understand something. These books are all about 'Phil Alman'. Are they novels, or are they autobiographical stories?"

This was a question that I detested, and I imagine most writers do also. "I take some real-life situations, people, and feelings and make up stories from there. Although some are just completely made up. Which is only for me to know."

"As your prisoner—"

"Guest"

"As your prisoner, your propensity toward hurting people is obviously of great concern, even if it is fictional. Though your predilection toward younger women gives me confidence that my virtue at least is safe."

I knew that Rachel was trying to get my goat. But I liked my goat, and I wasn't giving it away. "That's why it's called *fiction*. But think what you want."

She gave me an eye roll worthy of one of my fictional young female paramours and got back to work on my books. I liked the yin and yang of our discussions. I write in a vacuum, and nobody else is a party to it. I know many, if not most authors, run their stuff by friends and family and other writers to get feedback to hone their work. I never have. But having someone like Rachel, with her smarts, education, and experience, was beneficial, and I liked how she didn't hold back even though she was my guest/prisoner. I've always liked strong women, despite what my books may suggest.

When we weren't talking about my books or literature in general, I found, surprisingly, that we had a good deal in common, as Dan Lee had intimated. You could take the girl out of the early 1980s Philly but you couldn't take early 1980s Philly out of the girl. She liked drinking (expensive wine and bourbon, not beer, but still), classic rock music (okay, more Jackson Browne than Mick or Elvis), and old movies (we both especially loved classic noir of the '40s and '50s), and she could swear like a sailor yet still sound eloquent.

It's a funny thing when a heterosexual man is in close confines with a heterosexual woman. Despite yourself, if there's an intellectual connection and some mutual physical attraction, the pheromones start shooting off all over the place. Even at our advanced ages. Given that I was holding Rachel Arison against her will, however, the pheromones that I shot mostly did not land on target.

I allowed Rachel to communicate with her office and a couple of acquaintances at least once a day, making sure that I saw every word that was being sent. She told them that a family crisis caused her to be on an unexpected hiatus, and I suppose, because of her many years of loyal service to Bryce Douglas, no one questioned her, and all wished her good tidings. I wondered what it would be like to be that respected by your colleagues. As a sole practitioner, I never got such love. Only disjointed ramblings from Dan Lee for which I was paying him generously.

****

"Whom do you read, Phil?" This was Rachel at noon that following Friday, having been my guest for over ninety-six hours. I was surprised that she wasn't more frightened of me. Or frightened at all. It made for a more pleasant conversation, but it was almost emasculating.

"My tastes run the gamut. In the crime fiction genre, I like some of Elmore Leonard's stuff, though he gets redundant. Walter Mosley. The classics, Hammett, Chandler, and Cain. Some others here and there. I'm not going steady with anybody though."

She laughed. "I play the field too. Those whom you mentioned are first-rate."

"As opposed to my third-rate material?"

"You're solidly second-rate." She stated this as a fact, not to be funny or mean. "There are moments in all of your books when I think, hey, this lunatic really gets it. Then you meander. But why no favorite female authors? Are you really the misogynist you play in your books?"

I felt chastened and got defensive. "Gillian Flynn's *Gone Girl* is as good a mystery novel as I've read in a long time. But in general, I don't love chick lit or Brit lit. Too effete for me."

"Dude, this faux macho bravado is setting you off course in life and literature."

"And you can set me straight?"

"As a human being, I think that train has already left the proverbial station, Phil. But as a writer, yes, I think that I can help make your books more favorable to women and thus more publishable. Maybe not by Bryce Douglas. But by good mid-level houses." She hesitated when I must have shown consternation on my face. "But yes, under these extraordinary circumstances, I think that I can get you a deal with BD without too many questions asked."

"Why aren't you more scared of me, Rachel? Angry even?"

To her credit, she looked me square in the face. "Phil, to be honest, you seem like a nice enough person. I like people who like books and you like books. We went to school together. I don't think you'll harm me. But I'm not sure enough about that not to do your bidding. I know how frustrating the publishing world is for newbies. It's much worse now than ever with almost all of the smaller houses going under. Like you experienced with your two publishers. If I weren't being held captive, you might even say that I'm rooting for you."

I didn't know if Rachel was trying to disarm me with these kind words. Figuratively and literally. But whatever her motives, it was working, and I almost felt like crying. If I wasn't so damn faux macho. "Well, thanks, Rachel. I'm sorry to have had to do this. But make no mistake, if you don't get me a book deal, it won't end well for you. I've hurt people for way less than having a dream quashed." I wondered if she believed me. I wondered if I believed me.

****

Fail to plan. Plan to fail. That's what they say, and I've proven the mantra true. I don't plan well. In my life. In my relationships. In my job. Or in my writing. As to the latter, I just usually start writing with no outline or idea where things are going to go. In my mind, it adds to the suspense because, along with the reader, I have no clue how things are going to turn out.

So, it is not surprising that I ran an under-planned kidnapping. Here we were in a shack in the Pennsylvania boonies. But I was keeping myself a prisoner as much as Rachel. I couldn't work. Go out. See anyone. How stupid. I still got emails almost daily from prospective clients. I wasn't financially able to retire yet. Maybe I'd get a big book deal out of this and maybe I wouldn't. That's a risky proposition on which to live the last quarter of one's life.

And if my next book was to be a fictional version of my abduction of Rachel Arison, it couldn't be a one-act one-scene, two-person play in a cabin. How boring.

****

"This is *King of Comedy*, Phil." My hostage and I calmly discussing my ransom later that day.

"What do you mean?"

"This whole set-up. It's like that '80s film. Martin Scorsese, DeNiro, Jerry Lewis?"

"I know the movie."

"The plot is the same. You're kidnapping an influential person who you think will give you an entrance to the world of fortune and fame. Only instead of showbiz and comedy, it's publishing and noir."

"Making me 'The King of Noir'? It's not exactly the same, but okay, maybe the movie gave me a subconscious idea. So what? Books and movies borrow from each other all the time. It's not plagiarism."

"I didn't say that it was. But things don't always work out like they do in the movies, Phil."

"Gee, thanks for that insight, Mom." At that split second, I remembered Dan's note about Rachel's possible Mommy fetish.

But she had a point. This escapade was following *The King Of Comedy* script a little too closely. I'd have to shake things up somehow. "Should we consummate the relationship to give the story a little extra spice?" I was kidding, but she wasn't sure of that.

"No."

"Then what can we do to liven things up?" We looked at each other glumly, not unlike an old married couple with nothing new to add to the relationship. Outside the shack, it was beginning to snow, but my weather app only called for a coating, so I was not concerned about getting snowed in. Then, I heard the buzz of a text come through on my phone.

—*Mistah Phil. Stop. Been trying to leach you. Stop. That rady Lachel's niece Aryssa found murdered Sunday night. Stop. Just lead about it on my phone, didn't know if you knew. Stop.*— Translated: Rachel's niece Alyssa had been murdered several nights ago.

Only Dan would type out a text like an old-fashioned telegram, in broken Chinese no less. Was it insane? For sure. And obviously disturbing news.

I looked around the shack. It had a basement with no windows in which Rachel had been sleeping, with a door that locked from the outside. I could accommodate my guest in that room with little or no concern of her escaping if I ventured out. Rachel looked at me with concern, seemingly reading my mind. But I'm no poker player and my mind was not exactly Greek mythology; it wasn't very hard to read. More like a Dr. Seuss book.

I can't hurt women. It doesn't make me a saint in the city or in rural Pennsylvania, and candidly, that inability possibly cost me some hookups. A lot of chicks seem to enjoy getting hurt, as they've told me. I'm just saying. If Rachel were a dude, I would have no problem locking him away down there. But I could not do it to her. She was a blameless victim in all this, and I still had a ripple of conscience and chivalry rippling through me somehow.

"What is it, Phil?" Also, Rachel was twice as smart

33

as I, and I understood that I could not pull the wool over her eyes on pretty much anything.

"Rachel, I got a message from my IT guy. And friend. I'm very sorry to tell you this, but your niece Alyssa appears to have been murdered a few days ago."

I did not read Rachel as a tough broad necessarily, but she had lived in two tough towns, working in a tough industry, and she reacted toughly, not showing much emotion. She nodded a time or two, took a deep breath, and reacted pragmatically. Maybe that's what big-time executives did.

"It's not overly surprising, Phil. It's sad, very sad. But Alyssa ran with a rough crowd and had some bad habits. She was twenty, I think, full of life and promise as a young girl, but it all unraveled in high school. Running away from home. Rehab, I think. She eventually graduated and aced the SATs but went to Temple for only one semester. She's my baby sister's kid. We weren't close. I haven't spoken to Karen or Alyssa in several years. I would like to go to the funeral to pay my respects, but I understand that under the circumstances, that will not be possible. I hope you will at least allow me to send a card, maybe some flowers." At which point, Rachel Arison, tough New York book boss, heaved a heavy sigh and broke down like a baby.

I pondered my options. There were some, but I knew the course I was going to take. I was too soft. "I could hold you here. But I'm not a very good kidnapper." Which is true, as I had tried and failed in one of my previous adventures. You're going to have to buy the entire set to know which one. "I could take you with me, Bonnie and Clyde style, as we hunt for the bad guy. After all, that's part of my job. Or keep you here and have you succumb to my worldview, Patty Hearst style. But you're no outlaw, and you're no sheltered daddy's girl. You're a brilliant, accomplished woman, and I don't think that I can pull it off, to be quite honest about it."

She answered immediately, as if this, too, was anticipated. "Phil, I somehow feel complicit in all this. I am a small cog in the giant wheel of publishing, but that wheel has quashed the hopes and dreams of many a good writer, as we have almost completely shut out the unknown, unagented author with our unrelenting mergers and acquisitions." Here she paused, either for dramatic effect or to decide what to do. "Phil, we were teenagers together. I know we weren't exactly friends, but I don't know anybody else from high school. I felt like I had outgrown all of that, and that is easy to do when you've had success in Manhattan. I want to help you. Your books are good. Not necessarily slam-dunk major publishing house good, but they, or at least most of them. have that potential with a little careful editing and honing.

"I don't have any close friends, Phil. Or as this tragedy has reminded me, any close family. If I am honest with myself, it's not because I moved to New York or that I recently moved back to Philadelphia. It's me. I am a closet misanthrope." She smiled. "As opposed to an in-your-face misanthrope like you." It was meant as a joke, but its accuracy still stung. "If you let me go, I will help you get published. But on your own merit. Let's focus on this next book, and together, we will make it Bryce Douglas material. Of course, I will use my connections and influence to help get it published, but in the end, I don't think you would be satisfied with that. I—"

"Oh, but I would."

"No, in the end, I don't think so. I've gotten to know you a little bit, Phil Allman. Your pride would make you think that you only got ahead through criminal intervention. We are going to work together, whereby the decision-makers at Bryce will want to publish your novels with no threats needed. You still need someone like me to get them to read it, though, of course. And maybe nudge it along as your advocate. But Phil Allman's next book is going to be on bookshelves, where such things still exist, all over the world."

It was quite a speech. Delivered with seeming sincerity. She could run for office with that brand of enthusiasm. Was it fake? To simply get her out of a jam? Making her the perfect femme fatale for this story? Or was it the genuine article? A woman throwing out a rope to save a man mired in quicksand. I've gone through a lifetime, and nine books of female betrayal. It was the essence of noir.

"Phil, you are going to have to trust someone," she said, reading my mind once again, "and trust a woman for once in your life. Despite all your noir teachings and tendencies."

And so, I did.

Chapter 5

So I let her go, driving her back to her posh Center City life and apartment, figuring that I'd have the police and/or the FBI arresting me for kidnapping any minute after I got home.

Those next few days back at my apartment in Northeast Philly were nervous, as I resigned myself to my fate of spending the fourth quarter of my life in prison. Respectable, responsible women like Rachel Arison do not allow strange men to abduct them off the street and keep them in some hellhole out in the hinterlands. I was going to be incarcerated soon, spending what's left of my children's inheritance on lawyers. I didn't run away and hide or arm myself to the teeth for a Mexican standoff with the authorities. I was anxious, but at peace with what I had done. I wanted to fulfill a dream, and it backfired.

Except Rachel Arison did not have me arrested. Nor did she even block me from her phone. I got a text saying that her niece's funeral was sad, but that it was nice in a way to reconnect with some family members whom she had not seen in a good while.

Ain't that peculiar, to quote Mr. Marvin Gaye? A few days later, she asked via text how my book was coming. Maybe the lesson is that if you trust women and treat them well, they won't turn on you.

Or more likely, I just got fucking lucky.

We texted back and forth sparingly, during which she said that the police hadn't made any arrests for her niece's killer, and she wanted to know how I would handle the case. Rachel said she wasn't overly confident in the small-town police handling things, in that Alyssa lived in a suburban Philadelphia hamlet called Souderton. She also requested that I send her pages when I got further along with my novel.

Was she setting up a tit-for-tat? A boob for a book as it were? Would she help me with my novel if I helped to find her niece's murderer? Fair questions that I thought better than to ask over the phone (knowing, for example, how intrusive an IT guy like Dan could get), so I suggested we get together for lunch. It was already veering toward Thanksgiving, and things would be getting mighty crowded downtown, so I suggested we meet for lunch the Tuesday before. She then suggested Benny's, an upscale deli on Chestnut Street, a couple of blocks from her apartment. Given that she kept me out of jail for ten to twenty, I didn't try to negotiate a closer rendezvous, and of course, I would treat.

****

I took SEPTA downtown since the El stopped a couple of blocks away on Market; driving into Center City was stressful and parking was crazy expensive. Plus, it was a nice brisk day, and walking around, once I arrived, downtown was kind of fun, gawking at the cute secretaries and envying the well-dressed execs.

Benny's was an old-school deli, with a pickle bar, egg cream sodas, and corned beef juicy enough to flood the nearby Schuylkill River. Which is what I got, corned beef on rye with brown mustard, fries, and a

Coke (I'm a health nut), and Rachel got a Caesar salad and water. She was looking fetching for a recent hostage, in a lovely green sweater and tight, expensive jeans. I just threw on a button-down shirt and jeans, which for me is getting dolled up.

"Your work fascinates me, Phil. The whole P.I. thing. I've only lived it vicariously through movies and books. Is it like that?" We were seated at a big red booth near the front of the restaurant, close enough to the door to feel the cold breeze when people came in and out.

"No, it's way more mundane. Most of it nowadays is video surveillance, usually investigating for insurance fraud or cheating spouses. Guns are never drawn, fists rarely fly, hearts are never, or at least not frequently, broken." Thinking of my beautiful and sweet second wife, Marci.

After our food came, Rachel proposed the tit-for-tat. But she added a wrinkle, something middle-aged women often loathe to do. "I'd like to be part of it. Help you out with your investigation. Like the molls in the forties flicks."

"Rachel, I don't think—"

"Yeah, Phil, this isn't a request. I'm telling you." The mommy thing coming out? I had no choice but to hire her as an unpaid intern. "I have kept myself buried in my work and my books, Phil. It's time that I start connecting with the human race again. Maybe by helping you, you can help me with this. Isn't that what friendship is? Two people helping each other when they need it?"

To those of you rolling your eyes, scoffing at the notion that Rachel Arison, recent hostage, would help her kidnapper, I have a simple message: Fuck you. I happen to be a nice person. Rachel saw that. She was freely helping me with my book, and her offer was genuine. So get over yourself.

"I need to tell you something, Rachel. This isn't a cozy novel scenario where a man and a woman join forces to take down an evildoer. It won't be like that. I'm not that guy. I use whatever means necessary to perform my job. Meaning unscrupulous methods, violence, whatever. This isn't *Manhattan Murder Mystery,* two frightened nebbishes scurrying around looking for clues. I'm not scared of anyone. If I need to beat the clues out of someone, I do it. Are you sure you still want to be a part of that? Also, I don't work for free. So somebody is going to need to pay me to work on this."

She looked crestfallen and more than a little angry. She already had delusions of being an Agatha Christie character. "Phil, I will be honest. I am not a fan of brutality. Not by the police, not by private investigators, not by anyone. Also, as far as paying, I think that if I get your book on the market, and you don't have to spend the rest of your life in jail for kidnapping me, that ought to be payment enough. I am shocked and hurt that you would even ask me to pay you under such circumstances. My niece was just murdered!"

Rachel was right, of course. On all of it. Still, I didn't want to do the boy/girl detective partner thing, either in fiction or in real life. Dennis Lehane pulled it off for a few books. I mostly didn't want someone looking over my shoulder in moral judgment over my, well, let's call them tactics. "I just don't think it would be a good idea. You know, the whole seeing how the sausage is made thing. It isn't pretty."

"What if I insist?"

She obviously had me in a precarious position. "If you insist, I'd say, welcome aboard to Phil Allman Private Investigations. As an unpaid intern."

"I accept. With a few conditions." Oh, here we go. "I have a demanding, full-time career. That comes first." Didn't I just tell her I didn't want or need her help? "Second, if you are involved in any illegal or immoral activities during your investigation, I do not want to know about it." Illegal and immoral activities are part of my job description. "But I also want to be apprised of all developments in the case. I would like to use whatever insight and intelligence that I have to help." I guess it couldn't hurt to bounce ideas off someone more intelligent. I have often done that with Dan Lee, but of course, he is insane. "I won't ask you if you agree. Because you have to agree." The mommy thing? "So, what's our first step, boss?"

This was either going to go horribly bad or just very badly. "I begin by having Dan do a search. In this case, I would have him look at all records pertaining to Alyssa. Is her last name Arison?"

"Yes, both my sister Karen and I maintained our maiden names, and she never got married."

No Neanderthal reaction from yours truly. "Okay. He'd look at phone records, credit card purchases, web browsing, dating apps, social media activity, work information, driving patterns, etcetera. You can put your hands over your ears. Much of what he does is officially illegal, but it is the standard operating procedure, and I don't think twice about it. We are likely to find out things about your niece's life that you may not want to know. You okay with that, intern?"

The gravity of what I just said affected the gravity of her face, and her middle-aged countenance visibly sagged. "Yes."

"Okay. Dan's fees are expensive, but he is the best. If your guilt encourages you to chip in for any of this, I would be happy to absolve you of it."

"Don't worry. It won't."

And so it began. Allman and Arison Investigations. The former using his money, extensive experience, and expertise, and the latter using her smarts as absorbed by reading P.D. James. Let's see where this ride takes us, shall we?

Chapter 6

I tasked Dan Lee with running a full report on Alyssa Arison over Thanksgiving weekend. His report would include things that broke state and federal privacy laws and would give me a black eye with the ACLU. Also meaning that it was *mucho* expensive.

The manifesto Dan delivered was not especially flattering to Alyssa. She was actually twenty-three, had graduated from George Washington High School (in the upper part, figuratively and literally, of Northeast Philadelphia), and attended Temple, dropping out after a year, not a semester as Rachel had said. She had worked in various retail and restaurant jobs since she was sixteen, and had had a good number of lovers of both genders and all ages and races over the last five or so years of her sadly short life. A regular weed smoker, but no excessive drinking or extensive use of anything harder, and she had not attended rehab as Rachel had thought. A profile not unlike many, if not most, of her generation. A very pretty young woman with a variety of hair colors and styles; not model material, and her figure was almost boyish, but certainly attractive. She had no problem getting all the dates that she wanted from Tinder, and she seemed to want plenty.

She moved out of her house before starting college, and had most recently been living alone in a small apartment, the third floor of a row house in a town called Souderton, just north and west of Philly. Then came the revelation. Since she was sixteen, she had been receiving incessant texts, then sexts from her good old uncle, Stanley Kret. Rachel's ex-husband for those of you keeping score at home.

Dan's practice was to call before emailing me his reports to give me the highlights. "Velly, velly strange."

"Knock it off, Dan. In English."

"Okay, sorry, Phil. Kret began texting, then sexting Alyssa while she was still in high school. For about a year, it seemed to be mutual, perhaps a teenage girl feeling her oats and exploring." As someone who had married a teenage girl barely old enough to vote, I kept the stones in my pocket from my glass house. "But after about a year, she insisted he stop texting her. She would block him, only to have him use burner phones and secondary, TextNow numbers to get through. He also contacted her on social media. He would not relent. The texts were mostly of the pleading, smooth-talking variety at first, only to progress to eventual threats. The police have looked into Kret as a suspect, but obviously, he hasn't been arrested, so perhaps they were just virtual threats from New York."

"Okay, thanks, Dan." The question now was whether I should tell this to Rachel. "Are there any other persons of interest?"

"There are a couple of guys whose relationships with Alyssa did not end amicably, so yes, and the police are also looking into them. I can send you more info when I do a deeper dive. This is just preliminary stuff." At which point, we said our goodbyes.

It would only upset Rachel if I told her, probably needlessly. On the other hand, if I didn't tell her and she found out, or Kret was subsequently arrested, she would not be pleased, and still could have me arrested for kidnapping her. I made the call.

"How is your, I mean, our investigation coming along, Phil?" This was the Monday afternoon after Thanksgiving weekend.

I gave her Dan's general rundown, then I felt compelled to tell her about Kret. She sounded neither surprised nor particularly upset, but these things are harder to gauge over the phone. "He is such a shit. What is our next step?"

Her making this a team effort was troubling. "The cops seem to be all over him. I will try to use my contacts in the Philly police force to find out more. But given that the case is in Souderton, and the NYPD had questioned Kret, I don't know how much information I will get that way. I may take the train up to Manhattan and have a talk with Kret myself."

"What do you mean 'have a talk'?"

"Look, Rachel, the less you know, the better. I am not planning to get rough with him or anything like that, but it has been known to happen. If you know about it, you could be considered an accessory, and you don't want to be part of the justice system, trust me. It's incredibly expensive, intrusive, and it could do untold damage to your life and career."

I thought the matter was settled when she said, "What if I insist?"

We both knew that she was holding all the cards. She could have me arrested for kidnapping whenever she wanted, and then it would be I who would be subject to the vagaries and expense of the justice system. "Rachel, I know you think that you might get a vicarious thrill by witnessing me interrogate Kret. Perhaps violently. I get it. But he doesn't know me. He knows you. If you're there, he will have you arrested in a New York minute, probably in New York."

There was hesitation over the phone, and I figured that was that. "I could always be hidden while you do it." This Ivy League, highbrow chick had balls, I will give her that.

I gave her the answer that I gave my kids, Jessica and Anna, when they had me cornered into doing something that I really didn't want to do. "Okay, we'll see." That seemed to mollify her, and we left it at that. Wanting to see her ex-husband manhandled and questioned showed a sadistic streak that I would not have guessed about Rachel Arison. I didn't know whether to be troubled or aroused.

Dan gave me more info on the other two guys, er, people (don't want to be accused of sexism) who had harassed Alyssa, though neither to the extent of Stanley Kret.

One was the guy that she bought pot from whom she met at Temple. Joe Cogan, now twenty-four, living with his parents in Hatfield, likely still selling dope. Joe and Alyssa dated two or three times from what Dan could glean, and Joe was none too happy when Alyssa started ignoring his texts and stopped using him as her source. No threats, but he badgered her for months, using a variety of numbers from which to text her.

And Steven Harrell, whom she dated until about a month ago. He worked as a car salesman at a local car dealership, twenty-eight, had a Bachelor's from Temple, and was living alone in an apartment in Lansdale. It seemed that he was simply broken-hearted when Alyssa turned away from him. Not that it matters (and it doesn't, I'm woke as shit), but Harrell was an African-American young man. Dan said that he had persisted in trying to call and text Alyssa, and unlike with Kret and Cogan, she did not block him on her phone, and he used his main cell number to contact her. One-way pleading types of texts. Been there, done that. It was quite the stretch to see him as a murderer, but Dan's job was to report what he found, and mine to do with it as I wished.

Dan of course couldn't see everything, namely people that Alyssa interacted with outside of the digital world, and of course, her murder could have been a random event. Lord knows that Philadelphia has recently been making its case as the murder capital of the United States, and some of that has permeated to the burbs. Our two most famous sons raped dozens of women (allegedly) and smacked the shit out of a comedian in front of the entire world. I'm telling you, it's in our Neanderthal water.

Alyssa was shot outside of the phone store at which she worked, and the only video (I didn't ask Dan how he was able to get it) blurrily showed a person in a hoodie shooting her once from about fifty feet away, no vehicle in the shot. It was at about seven-thirty at night on a Sunday night after the store closed, and Alyssa was not robbed. So, it would seem to have been personal, but who knew anymore?

Meanwhile, I was aware of the time slipping away. *The ticking of the clocks,* as Bob Dylan put it. I'm healthy, mentally (don't even) and physically. Not everyone my age is. Or even alive. But what was I doing with it? Not much. Not enough.

Was I going to chase down Stanley Kret and smack the shit out of him? With Rachel Arison in tow, no less? Yeah, probably. Was I going to fuck Rachel Arison, or anyone else for that matter, in the near future? No, probably not. Was I going to work on my relationships more with my sometimes overly independent children? Yeah, I always did, and gladly. Was I going to finish this book, the book that will either be bound for anonymity among the millions out there online on vendor sites, or have it published by a major house like Bryce Douglas, accomplished by abducting and threatening one of its Senior Vice Presidents? I still did not know. So, whether it's the beginning of the fourth quarter or sudden death overtime, was my fate just more of the same bullshit? Likely.

They say that writing is cathartic. Not fucking cathartic enough, baby.

If I was going to New York to hassle Kret, I knew that The Big Apple had major Covid restrictions, meaning that I'd probably have to get a hazmat suit just to be allowed out on the streets. I'm vaccinated and boosted, but that's still not enough for some areas. Is it hysteria or rightful concern? By the time you read this, you may know.

I had Dan run reports on Cogan and Harrell, the other two guys who couldn't seem to let Alyssa Arison go. Not much germane on either. Cogan, as I expected, had a couple of minor run-ins with the law over his pot business, but otherwise, he was your garden variety Gen Z slacker and stoner. A good-looking girl like Alyssa can drive a man to act out of character, as I well knew, but his being a murderer was a long shot. I could talk with him and make threats (marijuana is still illegal in Pennsylvania, kids), and I would, if nothing else. Dan said that the police talked with him about Alyssa and left him alone after that.

Harrell's background was even cleaner. College grad, always employed, currently selling cars (well), close with his family, and seemingly lovesick over Alyssa Arison. Bro, I understand. (I say bro in the spirit of kinship, not as an African American allusion, so don't send me the email). An even longer shot.

Which left Kret. The whole creepy uncle thing was bad enough, but the violence against Rachel specifically made me angry. Okay, it's true that I gave Rachel chloroform and held her hostage in the middle of nowhere against her will, but I'm a nice guy. Can't you see the difference? Schlepping Rachel up to New York with me so she could watch me work on Kret sounded both bothersome and enticing in its own way. I enjoyed playing the hero for women. Fuck, I've written nine books about it.

Maybe I could try to turn it into a romantic getaway. I know that I had the whole abduction thing working against me, as well as an intellect and bank account significantly inferior to Rachel's, but you never know. She seemed like a lonely woman, and I think that she liked some things about me. Relationships have started with less going for them.

I'd have to get Dan to do an ultra-deep dive into Stanley Kret before we made such a trip. I wanted to hit him where he lived, both physically and emotionally, and some intel going in would help.

****

"I still love him, you know." This was Rachel on our way to New York on a late Wednesday morning, the first day of December. Sophisticated Manhattanite as she was, she did not want to take the train up, so she insisted on driving. The weather was perfect for such a trip, brisk and sunny. We were in her extremely well-appointed Lexus with enough leather to make any sadist orgasmic. "Even though he...wasn't very nice, it was his idea for the divorce, actually."

That wasn't the impression I got from Dan's report, but I was hearing it from the horse's mouth, so to speak, and she had no reason to lie. "He wasn't all bad, and despite everything, you grow used to somebody, do you understand?" I did, all too well, having lost two wives along the way, but still, I didn't know how this lovely, brilliant woman could be in love with a loser and an abuser. Takes all kinds, I guess, is the answer.

I wasn't used to being a passenger, and I had to hold myself back from commenting on Rachel's driving a few dozen times as we made our way up the not-too-busy New Jersey Turnpike early that afternoon to the scary Lincoln Tunnel and then over to Kret's place in Chelsea. Dan told me that Kret was working as a print salesman in the city and that he usually got home by four, although not always, and we were taking a chance with this whole expedition. I told Rachel to pack a bag with a couple of days' clothes and essentials, just in case. Hotels wouldn't be astronomical mid-week if we needed to get one. Or as Rachel put it, "two rooms, we each pay our own way".

Dan's report showed that Kret had held about a dozen different sales jobs over the past decade, never earning close to what Rachel did. His second wife, Andrea Goldsmith, was a paralegal at a posh Manhattan firm, and she earned a good deal more than Kret. On top of this, Dan reported Kret was short, overweight, and balding. What was his appeal? Kret was not close to his family of which an elderly mother and older brother were all that was left. He had no serious hobbies or vices to speak of. He was just some guy. Did he have big dick energy? I would not be asking that of Rachel.

I had taken SEPTA to Center City, then walked over to Rachel's apartment building (she did not let me come upstairs) and from there we retrieved her car from a parking lot that cost about the same as my rent every month. The rich really are different from you and me, thanks FSF.

We left at about one, and traffic wasn't bad at all until we got off the turnpike exit and approached the famous tunnel. There, things were pretty backed up. I had meant to ask Rachel to pull into the Vince Lombardi turnpike stop before we got into the city so that I could take a pee break, but since I didn't have to go very badly at the time, I held my tongue. That was a mistake.

"Why are you squirming around like that, Phil? Nervous? Ants in your pants?"

Totally embarrassed was I, and I did not reply, but tried to sit still until we were on the other side of the tunnel, and I could ask Rachel to pull over near a restaurant or something. There was nothing I could do about it, sitting in the long line of cars headed toward the tunnel except squirm. When we finally saw the light at the end of the tunnel, I told Rachel my problem, and her mommy instinct kicked in. "Oh, poor Phil. We'll find you a place to go soon." And she did, parking her car next to a hydrant on Tenth Avenue as I headed to a

Freeze Out (one of my best books, buy it) in the form of a little diner. The day was cold but dry, so jogging the half-block toward the entrance was easy. The pretty Greek (I assumed) hostess asked me how many, but I didn't stop to answer and scurried toward the restrooms at the back of the restaurant. Oh, what a relief it was (another old-time cultural reference)!

From there, Rachel meandered her way to Kret's building near Twenty-Sixth and Ninth. It was four-fifteen, and Dan texted me that it seemed like Kret was home. "Do you have a plan on how to do this, Phil?" Rachel asked as we headed toward his apartment house after parking the car in an incredibly expensive lot.

I did and did not, but just told her to follow my lead, and she did. I was in a black parka and jeans. Rachel was in a bright yellow winter coat and tan slacks. I probably should have told her to wear something less conspicuous, but there was nothing to do about it at that point.

On one hand, you couldn't just waltz into Kret's building, but on the other, this wasn't a doorman and tight security type of place, so we stood outside the building waiting for a resident to get buzzed in, and then follow him or her. It was a her, an elderly lady of about seventy (though as I neared that age, I hated the pejorative "elderly" more and more), and we followed her into the elevator. Kret's apartment was on the fifth floor. The lady got off on three.

"Are you nervous, Rachel?"

"Nope." And she appeared calm. I, on the other hand, was a wreck. I was pumping out sweat from my armpits and crotch (which, due to a bad moment making my way toward the diner restroom also had a urine-smelling tinge), and I was scared. I was in a strange city in a strange apartment building that, lax security or not, had video surveillance at its entrance at least, and I was perhaps going to commit a felony by roughing up some guy whom Rachel now said she still loved. What the fuck was I doing there? "Are you, Phil?"

"Nope." The stoic gentleman always. "But I'm not sure that we should be here." At which Rachel let loose.

"Listen, buddy. You owe me. Now do what you do, and let's see what we can find out."

I still hadn't figured out for Rachel the voyeur how to watch me do what I do other than to tell her to wait out in the hall and peek in. We could have waited until Kret went out someplace, but I wanted to get this over with, and the inside of his apartment seemed as good a place as any to get 'er done.

Kret's apartment was 503, and close to the elevator. Good for escape, bad for the number of witnesses who could be within earshot. We walked over and my heart was hammering. I debated whether to knock first to allow me to enter his apartment peacefully, but I figured that no New Yorker would open his door to a stranger. I motioned for Rachel to move out of the way and then I shouldered the locked door open and burst inside while Rachel hid the best she could out in the hall.

Kret was in a button-down business shirt and slacks, sitting in front of a laptop with Sports Center on TV in the back of the room. He appeared to be working and, surprisingly, not overly startled when he saw me at the door. I guess in New York nothing surprises you. He tried not to act scared and so did I as he stood up and said, "Who the fuck are you?" I couldn't fault him for swearing at that moment, right? Kret was about five-six and chubby, so I was wildly confident that I could kick the shit out of him if I so chose, but I so chose to hold off until he answered some questions.

"Never mind who I am. Tell me about Alyssa Arison and make it fast." I was afraid that a neighbor would have heard the door crash open, but being New York, they would probably just mind their own beeswax, an endearing expression used frequently by my lovely second wife.

"What about her?"

"Why did you stalk her? She was your niece, you fucking pervert." Said the man who married a girl just out of high school.

"I've been over this already with the police. Who I am going to call unless you leave right now!" I glanced toward the door and saw Rachel lingering, mostly out of sight.

After Kret's threat to call the police, which I took very seriously, I picked him up using his shirt for leverage and threw him, hard, against the wall that probably served as the border to his bedroom. He crumbled to the ground, moaned, and I felt a certain elation that I could still easily wreak such havoc. It's a guy thing. "I'm going to ask you again. Why did you stalk her?"

He saw that I was likely to do him more physical damage if he didn't answer as I hovered over him, so he said, "I loved her. Wrong or right, I loved her." And he teared up. I actually felt sorry for him at the moment, my empathy having heightened as I got older.

"O.J. loved Nicole too. Is that why you killed her?

Because you couldn't have her, and you didn't want anyone else to?"

The tears turned to outright sobbing, and I really started to feel bad for this schmuck. "I would never hurt Alyssa."

"Right. Just like you wouldn't hurt Rachel, huh?"

Kret stopped crying long enough to say, "I treated Rachel terribly. No excuse. But I didn't love Rachel." Ouch. That had to hurt my company's new unpaid intern as she listened out in the hall.

"And your second wife, Andrea? You seem to get off on hurting women."

Kret just shook his head. "I've been a bad husband. But I would never hurt Alyssa. Believe me or not. I don't know who you are or why you're here, but the NYPD already interrogated me at their station. I didn't bring a lawyer or anything because I had nothing to hide. Think what you want."

I felt like every second that I stayed in the apartment was another second before somebody inevitably called the cops. I could try to beat a confession out of Kret, something the NYPD supposedly doesn't do anymore, but I didn't think I would get one. I wasn't sure if he was innocent. But I wasn't sure he was not.

I rushed out of the apartment, and motioned for Rachel to quickly follow me as I headed toward the stairs rather than chance waiting for the elevator. I wanted to get the fuck out of that building as fast as I could. The great thing about New York is that once you're out on the street, you're fairly anonymous as you blend in with the other miscreants. We hustled to the outdoor parking lot where Rachel had left the Lexus, and she paid the attendant forty dollars (!) and he brought us the vehicle. Rachel gave him a two-buck tip, and we headed back toward the Lincoln Tunnel. A six-hour roundtrip for a two-minute interlude. I suppose some lovers traveled farther for even less time though.

When we were safely in her car with no police seeming to follow us, I said, "Well?"

"He's lying. And you barely fucking touched him." This was followed by three hours of silence as we drove back to Philadelphia.

In the silence, I began to think about what my misogynistic cousin Mick, whom you met in *The One You Never Seen Before,* said. He thinks women like guys who rough them up a little. I did not buy into that, but why did she still love Kret?

I have to give her credit. For someone who rarely drove, Rachel, after we inched our way out of Manhattan during rush hour, weaved in and out of traffic on the notoriously dangerous New Jersey Turnpike like a champ. Because she wasn't speaking and would not let me turn on the radio, my only entertainment was marveling at her smooth reflexes.

"Rachel, I understand that you're angry, but we did what we came to do. I broke into Kret's place. I threw him up against a wall. The police would have arrived any minute, and we should be glad that we got out of the building and out of the city without getting arrested."

She hesitated before speaking. I think because she learned long ago that the silent treatment was the most torturous way to treat a man. "We did not do what we set out to do. We did not get a confession. That was the whole point. I know you resent me, Phil. You resent my success. Back in high school and now. Well, let me tell you something. I am successful because I do what I set out to do. Unlike you, which is why you're a loser."

Ouch! The L word. Maybe she had a point, but I felt like defending my actions would just make things worse. My internal lie detector, which had served me well for many years, told me that Kret, dirtbag though he was, told the truth about Alyssa. That said, like all appliances and the human body, my lie detector's effectiveness had withered somewhat with age, and I did not trust it implicitly anymore.

Rachel did not use a GPS, and she surprised me by taking the Pennsylvania Turnpike directly from Jersey and getting off at the Trevose exit, meaning that she had to meander her way through what was her old upper Northeast neighborhood and my lower one. I figured she was going to drive right to Center City and have me take SEPTA to get back home, but she drove me directly to my apartment. When I gave her my address, she still did not use GPS. You can take the girl out of Northeast Philly, but you couldn't take Northeast Philly out of the girl.

It was approaching eight at night, and except for one turnpike restroom break, we hadn't stopped and had nothing to eat all day. Maybe Rachel had a huge lunch before we met, but I know my stomach was rumbling. I was starved. "Hey, would you like me to buy you dinner, Rachel?"

"No." The last thing I wanted to do was upset her further because of that little kidnapping escapade and all. She could still send me to prison for the rest of my life. So, I didn't say anything further, and when we got to my apartment building, she didn't say anything, and I just got out with the overnight bag that I had packed.

I turned on the lights as soon as I got in my place, not taking my coat off before throwing a Stouffer's lasagna (mmm!) in my microwave. I waited the full sixteen minutes to finish heating it up, expecting the knock on the door from Philly PD. But it did not come.

Chapter 7

I just could not figure women out. I know that's part of their appeal, but I did Rachel's bidding by jostling her ex-husband, yet she was angry at me because I didn't go far enough. The thing about beating confessions out of people is that, while it sometimes works (and it has for me), it usually doesn't, and even if people confess, it's often untrue just to get out of getting a worse beating. I went up to New York thinking that a little weasel like Kret would cry and babble out his guilt, but he was either more resolute than I had thought, or he was more innocent than I had assumed. Either way, I guess Rachel was right—we accomplished nothing, and as that goes, I guess my losing streak remained intact.

I asked Dan to get intel on Kret's second wife with no other avenues to pursue.

Except for the one that led to this entire ordeal. I had to work on this book and make it good enough for Rachel and her colleagues to accept and market it without reservation. It's not enough to get a book published; the marketing people had to believe in it and get it noticed online since brick-and-mortar bookstores have largely gone the way of the drive-in movie. A novelty that people talk about simply for its scarcity.

Sitting down to write fiction is hard. It's not a matter of composing pretty prose like most people think. You have to keep the story moving forward; have characters that are believable and likable (or unlikable); have those characters speak dialogue that rings true and have settings that make the reader feel they are there, but not so much as to bog the reader down with too much detail. Of those, I know my settings tend to be too spare, but even when I read a book, I often gloss over them because I don't really care how Sally's dress drapes over her bosom or how the gray sky looks like a burned-out frying pan. But that's just me.

Since my book was ostensibly following the current doings, I was glad Kret did not confess, to be honest about it. It kept the ball rolling as it were as to whodunit, the backbone of any mystery novel. I'm not going to detail my writing process because I know it's boring to read about, so I'll just say that I write in fits and starts, and I'm not as disciplined about it as the big boys. Perhaps if this was how I earned my living, I'd take it a little more seriously.

Anyway, Dan emailed over his report about Kret's second ex-wife. Andrea Goldsmith was a paralegal at one of Manhattan's more prestigious law firms, and earned a lot more money than you might think a secretary would, and certainly a lot more than Kret earned hawking printing services.

Andrea was forty-three, so significantly younger than Kret, who was fifty-five; she had no children or previous marriages and had a pretty active social life living in lower Manhattan. Pretty but not beautiful, a brunette with brown eyes and a nice enough figure. She wouldn't stop traffic, but you would definitely notice her at a cocktail party.

The most surprising aspect of Dan's report was

this: it was Kret who filed for divorce, not Andrea Goldsmith, even with the alleged abuse. I wondered to myself how Kret, a little, pudgy, unsuccessful, unattractive dork was able to attract and then marry two pretty, successful women like Rachel and Andrea Goldsmith. The knee-jerk answer is big dick, but there had to be something else. Was his very abusive nature appealing to them? I would have to broach that subject carefully with Rachel; I could be more assertive if and when I spoke with Goldsmith.

I emailed my pages to Rachel, and they did not impress her. "Your other books had passion, Phil, enough so that even if the writing wasn't Shakespearean, they held my interest because you seemed so interested in them. Does that make sense?"

It did, and she hit the nail on the head. Whether it's love or lust or anger, I usually write in spurts when my blood is up. My blood, like other things, wasn't up as long or as frequently as it was twenty years ago, and manufactured love or lust or anger comes off as fake.

But it did upset me how this Kret not only got primo women, but had them begging for more. As my cousin Mick told me, Charlie Brown isn't getting the little red-haired girl in the twenty-first century because she's off fucking some asshole while poor Charlie is left holding the flowers that he bought her in one hand and his dick in the other. I texted Rachel about it that Friday morning, thinking it might get my juices going.

—*Why Kret? Why did you stay with him? I don't get it.*— A fair and honest question, or so I thought.

—*Phil, that's none of your goddamn business, and it has nothing to do with Alyssa's murder. Do your job and stop prying into my life.*—

I always brought out the best in women.

****

I decided to call Andrea Goldsmith, Kret's second ex. Dan got me her number and more details. Born and raised in Brooklyn. Kret was her only husband, no kids. Allegations of abuse in the divorce files, yet again, it was Kret who filed. It had to be big dick energy, right? Had a very active post-marital social life, both hanging out with friends and dating from the usual apps. Not hard to find things to do and people to do them with if you're an attractive woman in Manhattan, though like with everyone, she had to slow her roll due to Covid.

I didn't know how or if Goldsmith tied into Alyssa's murder, but the thing about investigations is that you never knew. At worst, you might glean a nugget of information from someone.

I called her the morning after I broke in and entered Kret's apartment and assaulted him, crimes for which I would get many years in prison if caught. Thankfully, the NYPD seemed to have bigger fish to fry, and/or Kret simply didn't report the crime for whatever reason. Pride? Shame? Wanting to stay out of law enforcement's crosshairs?

As I expected, I got Andrea's voicemail when I called. Nobody picks up from an unknown number anymore, plus I knew she was at work. I left my name and number and said that I was investigating Stanley Kret, hoping she would cooperate out of spite. She did.

She called me at twelve-fifteen, which Dan told me was when she usually took her lunch break. "Mr. Allman, this is Andrea Goldsmith. How may I help you?"

Very professional and customer service-y, as one

might expect from an expensive New York paralegal. "Ms. Goldsmith—"

"Andrea."

"Andrea. And please, call me Phil. Your ex-husband is a peripheral part of an investigation, the nature of which I am not at liberty to discuss." I had no idea what that meant or why I said it, but it seemed like a lawyerly thing to say. "You were married less than three years. May I ask the reason for your divorce?"

"I don't want to go into detail, Phil, but let's blame it on irreconcilable differences as it states in the court documents."

"Right. I know those were the terms that the two of you agreed to, and that Stan asked for the divorce. Was there infidelity involved? Abuse of any kind?"

"I am sorry, Phil, but I would rather not say."

She was holding her cards close as one would expect of someone who worked in the legal world. "We have indications that Stan abused you but no police visits or verification. Do you care to comment?"

Dead air. "No. Is there anything else that you want to know?" Basically affirming what I had alleged.

"Do you know of an Alyssa Arison?"

More dead air, then "Yes." I was surprised at her acknowledgment.

"Ms. Goldsmith, Andrea, I know that you don't have to speak with me at all, and I appreciate your doing so. But if I wanted to pull teeth, I would have gone to dental school."

I was waiting for either a chuckle or the sound of her clicking off, and I got the former. "I don't know why you're asking, Phil, but yes, Stan seemed to have a little crush on what was his niece by marriage. It was pretty sick."

"So you knew about it."

"It's not like Stan hid it or that it meant anything. Alyssa was a hundred miles away and showed no interest back, so I thought if Stan was going to show interest in someone, having him do so with someone unattainable wasn't so bad."

Wow. I reiterate: women never ceased to amaze me. Here was this accomplished, attractive woman acknowledging that her ex-husband was the creepy uncle, and still it was he who wanted out of the marriage and not her. He must have a huge dick, though I did not ask Andrea nor would I ask Rachel. "The reason that I ask about Alyssa Arison is that she was murdered here in the Philadelphia area."

Silence. "Am I a suspect, Phil?"

I answered her honestly. "You're not a prime suspect, no."

"I know that you're a private cop. If the real cops want to speak with me, and they haven't, they know where to reach me."

At which point, she hung up. Had I learned anything? Only that women go for the oddest guys sometimes. But I was no closer to fulfilling Rachel's mandate to find Alyssa's killer than I had been when I woke up.

I, of course, could have done my due diligence and investigated the two dudes who stalked Alyssa. But I wasn't being paid for this job, and my instincts told me it would be a waste of time, and why waste my time when there was so precious little of it left? I could tell Rachel that my investigation, like that of the Souderton

Police Department, the NYPD, and others, had netted no results. What's the worst that she could say?

Chapter 8

"Phil, if you want to stay out of jail and get a publishing deal, I expect results." This was over the phone that same afternoon after my fruitless call with Andrea Goldsmith, and it was the worst that she could say.

I expected this reaction, and this time, I was prepared. "Rachel, I am not going to submit to your blackmail. Or your black male, if you know one." I thought she'd appreciate the pun with a chuckle, but as was usual lately, I was incorrect. I pressed on. "You came out to my cabin with me. You can't prove that you went involuntarily. We were seen at the Warwick and at Curly's and Benny's, and I could convince anyone that what we had was a romantic rendezvous." I let that settle in. "As far as my publishing deal, you said yourself that you could not unilaterally get me a contract and get Marketing behind it. And anyway, I've lived a half-century plus without a major book deal, and I can live the next quarter-century plus without one. I've resigned myself to a life of quiet desperation, and I've gotten quite accustomed to it."

So there it was. I de-fanged Rachel Arison. She did not reply for a full minute. "I would like you to visit me at my apartment, Phil. Yes, that would further verify that we have a consensual relationship as you pass through the doorman and video camera in my lobby. I have something to show you. Can you come by at around five? After which, I will treat you to a nice dinner."

Well, this was unexpected. I was invited to the apartment of an attractive, accomplished woman who lived in a de-luxe apartment in the sky. I was movin' on up.

****

I decided not to take public transportation to Center City this time because of the wind chill; it was in the teens. Plus, driving against traffic in the late afternoon usually isn't too bad, and, in fact, it was not. There are two major arteries to get downtown, either I-95 or I-76, which is known to visitors as the Schuykill Expressway and to Philadelphians as the SureKill. From my apartment, either one worked, but I took the Expressway for a change of scenery. You take Route 1 (which extends through the entire East Coast, by the way) South to get on 76 East which is the Schuylkill, and Rachel's apartment was closer to it than it was to 95. It was a pale winter sun that partially blinded my middle-aged eyes much of the way as it approached sunset in the opposite direction, but as I suspected, traffic wasn't too bad, and I got there in less than an hour. Parking was a killer, but I wasn't sure that Stanley Kret was. I assumed that was Rachel's agenda, but it's always a precarious feeling to meet someone when they know what they want to talk about, and you walk in clueless. I think that's how most men think about marital conversations.

Rachel's building on Rittenhouse Square was posh, as I figured—a doorman with gold braids on his jacket and everything. I had to check in at the security desk, and Rachel had left my name as a bonified visitor. I was wearing a nice business shirt and sweater combo with khakis and off-brand Hush Puppies, so I felt confident. I even splashed on a little cologne because you never knew.

Her apartment was on the seventeenth floor, and I knocked nervously. I was a man in the final quarter or so of life and I still got anxious visiting a chick. Is that cute or pathetic?

She answered, and was wearing a red and gold sweater, jeans, and casual shoes. Meaning she looked nice but not I want to jump your bones nice. This, I inferred, was a business meeting, and for once, I was on the money.

She led me into her place. I don't know styles of furniture and I'm not researching it, but everything looked clean, nice, and expensive. Paintings on the wall, plants on tables and windowsills, little knickknacks throughout, things that most heterosexual men would never think of. The room smelled like vanilla ice cream, and suddenly I felt hungry.

"I invited you here because I want to show you something." At which point she did *not* take off her sweater. That's another kind of book. On an end table was an unmarked file folder, and she picked it up, handing it to me. She gestured for me to sit, and I chose the plush dark green loveseat, and Rachel planted herself on the adjacent sofa of the same color and material.

I then opened the folder and was aghast, no other word, aghast at what was inside. A half-dozen eight-by-ten black and white photos of Rachel Arison with bruises and cuts on her face, a black left eye, and a swollen bottom lip. She appeared to be about five years younger than the woman who sat near me.

"You see, Phil, this is why I wanted you to be rougher with Stan. Not as revenge for what he did to me. But because this is how he treats women, and I am positive he murdered Alyssa. He obviously is not going to confess to the crime; he's not stupid by a long shot. And there may not be incriminating evidence. But he killed her, and he should pay the consequences."

Maybe Rachel read me like one of her books, I don't know, but in the moment, I agreed with her. If Kret was in the room, I probably would have beaten him to near death. I can't abide men who hurt women. At all.

"Rachel, I'm very sorry that this happened to you. And I don't disagree with anything you've said. But we live in a country of laws, and vigilante justice isn't justice. I'm sorry."

She nodded as if she expected this type of response. "I don't want you to hurt him physically anymore. I just want justice for Alyssa."

I gave her the only answer that I could. "I can investigate him further and see if I can find something to pin this on him. But it will be both difficult and unlikely at this point. The police forces with a lot more resources than I have were unable to do it." I suddenly wanted to leave Rachel's posh pad, feeling claustrophobic. And hungry. "Can we get dinner?"

"Phil, I imagine there are ways of planting incriminating evidence for a skilled, experienced investigator like yourself." Playing on my starving ego.

"There are. But I don't want to go there. I enjoy not being in prison."

"I imagine there are ways to do this where you would not risk that."

"You've read too many mystery novels, Rachel." I hesitated. "It is really difficult to plant evidence long after a crime has taken place. The police have already combed through everything. Anything planted now would be suspect. And likely tossed out by a good defense lawyer." I paused for dramatic effect. "However."

"Don't fuck with me, Phil. However, what?"

You can't take Philly out of the girl. "I'm aware of a case where a suspect's laptop was planted with child pornography. It is not difficult for someone like my IT guy Dan to do. Extremely illegal. But not difficult." I didn't say that it was one of my cases and I wanted someone to burn for another crime. It is in one of my previous books. Again, you may as well buy the entire set.

"Child porn isn't exactly a murder conviction, Phil."

"In a way, it's worse. Judges are really tough on pedophiles these days, rightfully so, and prisoners are way, way harsher toward pedos than killers. If Kret got five to ten, it would be like a life sentence for murder. You get your revenge, Alyssa gets some degree of justice, and Kret gets beaten and boogered for the rest of the decade."

Rachel ruminated. "And there's no way that it would come back to me? Or you, for that matter?"

"It's like betting on a ballgame. There are no sure things. But this is like Alabama playing Vanderbilt in football." I got a blank expression back. "Meaning it's as close to a sure thing as you can get."

She paused, then said, "Let's do it."

"Hold on a second. If I and my friend Dan commit this felony, there are going to be some conditions. First and foremost, no more threats about accusing me of kidnapping. Second, you will do everything in your power to not only get me a book deal but to use your influence to get Bryce Douglas to promote the hell of my next book. Obviously, I can't write up a legal contract with these terms. All I want is your solemn word."

At which point, Rachel reverted to what was probably her ten-year-old self, licked the palm of her hand, gestured for me to do the same, and then we shook on it. As binding a contract as I have ever signed.

****

Rachel and I walked the few blocks to Morgan's, an upscale steakhouse on Chestnut. It was early on a Thursday evening, and it wasn't so crowded that we needed either a reservation or fancy attire, but this was a pretty pricey place for yours truly. She was buying so I didn't sweat it. Knowing that her ex-husband would soon be in prison brightened Rachel's mood; I wonder if either of my exes would have felt similarly. One hopes not.

She ordered an expensive bottle of Italian red wine for us, sniffed the cork, and did the taste test thing, really getting off on being in control. Maybe the whole Mommy thing, I don't know. There was that low conversational buzz in the restaurant that one hears at expensive places, as opposed to the eateries I grew up visiting, where families yelled at each other at the top of their lungs, usually mine included. I ordered a filet medium rare with a salad and baked potato after Rachel ordered the same first. I wasn't used to being wined and dined, but I could grow used to it.

"Dan can really put illegal porn on Stan's phone and laptop?"

"Very easily."

"That's kind of unsettling. Pretty good idea not to make enemies." I nodded in agreement. "I'm excited about your book, Phil. I've never been involved in the spawning of a manuscript, only in the editing and approval or disapproval stage after it's been written. I don't have that creative gene."

"You know what Ernest Hemingway said? When asked what it takes to be a great writer, he replied, 'an unhappy childhood'. Maybe that's why."

Rachel grinned. "No, my childhood was not traumatic or even bad, but it certainly was not idyllic. I don't think anyone's is. Was yours?"

The busty waitress brought our salads and bread, and I took a gulp of wine. "I would rather not be psychoanalyzed at dinner. Let's just say that it was not idyllic either."

She gave me a gotcha click with her mouth and dug into her salad. "So you're writing a fictionalized version of our relationship? Is there any sex in it?"

I looked for a blush to come to Rachel's cheeks, but there was none. Was she trying to seduce me, Mrs. Robinson style? I took another gulp of wine and stammered a bit. "I don't know yet."

Then she winked and said, "All modern fiction needs some sex, Phil. You don't want to let our readers down." Wow. She was trying to seduce me! Here's to you, Mrs. Robinson! I think that knowing she was partly responsible for eventually putting Kret in prison set off her libido. You never knew what was going to turn a woman on.

And you never knew what was going to turn a man on either, especially at my age, but between the wine, the ambiance, Rachel's beauty and intellect along with the experiences that we shared, it was getting the old blood flowing, no blue pill necessary. Remember how at the beginning I was bemoaning everybody getting laid? That only happens during celibate times. And I was pretty sure that the times were a-changing.

****

I get creeped out when authors write detailed sex scenes. They're not erotic to me, they're just icky. So I'm not going to give y'all a play-by-play, go elsewhere for that. I'll just report that it had been a while, but the combination of wine and Rachel dissolved any performance anxiety I may have had. And it went well.

Was Rachel Arison, my intellectual and social better, not to mention my recent hostage going to be my girlfriend? Maybe so, kids, you're just going to have to wait to find out.

Chapter 9

So yeah, that happened. The next morning, I placed a call to Dan and gave him his assignment.

"Oh, Mistah Joe, I don't know. Do you rearry want me to put irricit porn on that fat man's phone? It's velly bad. And velly expensive."

"Dan, speak normally, goddammit. I know. I do feel a little guilty about it. But Kret may have killed Alyssa Arison, probably so, in fact. He sexted his niece, for God's sake. He beat the crap out of Rachel, and she showed me photographic evidence to prove it. The fact that he hasn't paid for any of his sins absolves me of feeling too much guilt. I know what I'm doing."

Dan hesitated. "Are you starting to have feelings for this Rachel Arison, Phil? I know that tone in your voice."

"It's irrelevant to the job I'm giving you. I'd say wait on doing it for a few days, though. If the police or I find Alyssa's killer with certainty and it's not Kret, I'll withdraw my request." After which, Dan asked about my kids, I asked about his family, yada yada yada, and we clicked off.

I didn't take implicating Kret falsely and having him imprisoned lightly. But we all rationalize our dirty deeds, and this one sure was not dirt cheap, but I felt it appropriate. Was I doing it to curry favor with Rachel, both romantically and ultimately financially, for when my book came out?

To again quote my lovely teenage ex-wife, yeah, duh.

Let me take this opportunity to discuss my lovely teenage ex-wife to those of you new to my saga, and who are appalled. I met Marci online as innocently as can be, and my connection with her had zero to do with her youth; the connection would have existed whether she was eighteen or eighty. Okay, maybe not eighty, but it was all on the up and up. I understand how you may disapprove. If a man my age had ventured to marry either one of my daughters, I, of course, would have discouraged him using any means necessary.

And to those of you new to my saga, my daughters, now in their mid-twenties, are Jessica, currently living in Pittsburgh and doing nicely, and Anna who moved back to Philly from New York about a year ago and doing very well thank you. My relationship with each has had its bumps along the way, but all was cool now. In case you're wondering, after much initial hesitation, both grew to love Marci and vice versa. It is always precarious when a white guy paraphrases MLK, but one should judge someone not by the age on their driver's license but by the content of their character. I am not going to spew epithets at you if we disagree on this one. I get it. You will meet Jess and Anna later as my tale unfolds.

****

Meanwhile, I was getting regular texts from Ms. Arison of the "did you do it yet?" variety; she was savvy enough not to put what "it" was in writing, but she couldn't wait for Kret to get arrested for illegal possession of child porn and the brutal punishment that would follow. Yet she said she loved him. Like the old song says, love is strange. I made a mental note to myself to a) not cross Rachel and b) not to let her fall in love with me, difficult as that would be for someone with my charisma.

She asked to visit my apartment that weekend to work on the book and I inferred perhaps for a roll in the hay, but one could never be sure. "Yeah, Rachel, I'd love to get together. But not here."

"What's the problem, Phil? Are you secretly married? Or have a girlfriend? Or boyfriend? It's cool. I'm open-minded." I think she was joking, but humor wasn't her strongest asset.

"No, no skeletons in the closets, either. Look, I'm just embarrassed about my place. It's not terrible or anything. But it's not nice. And it's not clean. And you can say that you don't care or that I'm being silly, but I've seen your place. And mine (I looked around at the Salvation Army-level furniture and dust mites that kept me company) isn't presentable to a woman like you. You can take that as a compliment, I guess."

She paused. "I do think you're being silly because I don't care. I recognize that men and women have different aesthetic standards and that you're less well-off than I am. But I recognize that you have a certain amount of pride and I respect that, Phil. Do you want to come over here on Sunday?"

How do I say the following without making her feel unimportant? I suppose by just telling her the truth. "Listen, this has nothing to do with you. But in the fall and at least the first part of winter, Sundays for me are football days. It's just an interest I have which may seem trivial to you, but there it is."

I thought she'd flip. The woman who did not press kidnapping charges, who was helping me to become a successful author. and with whom I made love, did not flip. "Phil, I understand. Stan was the same way. We all have our interests. If football is yours, that's completely fine. I would invite you over tomorrow (Saturday), but I fell way behind on my work due to my recent incarceration, so I have to catch up. Let's talk next week."

And she hung up. Was she really okay with me blowing her off to watch football? Someday they'll invent a female-to-male translation robot.

I called the girls over the weekend (before football) to catch up and to let them know that their father just might have a major book deal in the works.

My call to Jessica was breezy. She said, "That's nice." and then talked about her trials and tribulations in the Steel City for an hour. That's not a put-down—we are all self-absorbed. I mean I'm talking about myself ad nauseam in this novel, right? Jess is pretty, blonde, very smart, very sensitive, and takes things very seriously, but she still has a good sense of humor. She wasn't being dismissive about my publishing possibility, but she had heard these Ralph Kramden delusions of grandeur before.

Anna is the intense, serious one. "That's awesome. When does your book come out?" Good question.

"I'm still writing it. I just happened to meet someone who's an important player in the publishing world, and she said she'd give it her priority. She read my other books and said they had promise."

Skeptical but trying to be positive, she said, "Great. Let me know when it comes out, and I'll buy it."

Meaning I'll believe it when I see it, but I'm the one who planted the seed of cynicism in the girls, so I could hardly fault them now that it flowered. Anna now had a steady boyfriend (Jess was "taking a break") and was making more money than I ever had. A pretty brunette, she was sweet, but you didn't want to get in her way.

I wrote a little more over the weekend. The writers' books all warned about the sloppy middle, meaning the big chunk of a book between the fast beginning and the climactic ending. You can pick up a novel from last week, last year, last century, it doesn't matter—they almost all suffer from the sloppy middle. Where the writer pads his (or her) word count and keeps things afloat until the mad dash to the end. Do you know what I mean? (Ironic self-deprecation in case you couldn't tell).

On my football Sunday, Rachel texted me she had to go up to Manhattan for some meetings that week, but that she'd try to call when she got back.

How does one try to call exactly? We've all heard the phrase. You can try to climb Mount Everest. Or try to mount a sexy actress. Worthy, arduous endeavors replete with obstacles and bushes and brambles along your course.

But try to call? When I was a boy, you had to put your finger in a hole (mind out of the gutter, pervert), and dial seven and then ten numbers. Now to call someone whom you know, you literally only have to press a button. There's nothing to "try". A monkey could do it. Or a baby.

So, when someone says they'll try to call, they mean they won't call, but they *tried*. Desperately made a valiant effort. You can't get upset with someone who does that. It is passive aggression at its finest. But by choosing my football Sunday over Rachel Arison, I made my bed, and I'd have to sleep in it alone, likely from here to eternity.

I kept at it with my book, though. I had made it to midfield, but Rachel's giving me the brush was like a bad quarterback sack, pushing me back to my thirty. Further to go but still within striking distance. I know that I promised no more football metaphors, but I am mired in the sloppy middle, so fuck off.

Her text also encouraged me to keep writing, which in fact was encouraging. Reading about someone writing is boring, so I won't dwell on the chasms of creative purgatory.

I had no incentive at this point to find Alyssa's real killer any more than O.J. did to find Nicole's. Kret was going to be in prison soon, so justice was likely served. The NYPD didn't care, the Souderton cops and their affiliates didn't care, Rachel no longer cared, so why did I? I was falling into the trap of mystery novels where the hero (that's me) continues to work on a case when he's not getting paid, and nobody else gives a shit. I hated that in books and movies because that's not how life works.

Alyssa's pretty face, however, stayed with me during football Sunday. Kret's denial rang true to me. I have no tolerance for creeps or woman beaters, and I had no qualms or guilt about putting him away for a long time. But that still meant that Alyssa's murderer, if not Kret, would skate. Could I live with that?

****

"Hey, Toke." This was me on the phone that Sunday evening before the Football Night in America game came on. I dubbed Brandon Johnson "Toke" not because of his propensity to smoke weed, which he did not, but because he was the token black detective at my Philly PD precinct many years ago.

"Hey, Cartman." Brandon calling me the name of a cartoon resident racist.

"Were you able to find out anything?" I had texted him before the Eagles game early that afternoon to see if he could find out anything about Alyssa Arison's murder. He had retired from the force a few years earlier, but still had many ties to people in the know, and I wanted to give the girl's death due diligence.

"I tried, Phil. The case is out of Souderton, so I was asking people to ask other people, and you know how reliable third-handed information is. I did find out that it's being labeled "unsolved" and not "cold", so it's active. Word is her uncle is the primary person of interest, but they can't pin anything on him."

I still had not had Dan do the child porn trick, so Kret was still living free and easy up in New York, likely with a replacement door and a very bad back, unaware that his life as he knew it was about to end. "Any other possible suspects?"

"They're looking into past boyfriends who had been aggressive via text, but no other solid leads. You know how it goes. Once you're out of the house, it's hard to get back in." Meaning once a cop retires, he's not privy to the skinny.

"It's a good thing they were using affirmative action, Toke, or else you never would have made detective with your watery interrogation skills." That's called a joke, I'm woke. Brandon was an A-plus detective, and everybody knew it.

My resources were way more limited than those of the NYPD, Philly PD, and Souderton PD. I'm brilliant, yes, but it was unlikely that I was going to find out anything they did not or would not, even if I were more focused on it than they. For all the recent talk of defunding the police because of systematic racism (which is real, don't kid yourself), if people knew how many felonies were never solved, the demand for defunding or "reimagining" the police would spread beyond young, woke urbanites, and spread out to mayonnaise-eating, chardonnay-drinking white suburbia.

I watched football for ten hours that Sunday, not feeling the least bit guilty of being a couch potato or rebuffing my would-be girlfriend. A man has the right to chill and be by himself. I just hope I won't be doing that the other six days of the week for years to come.

Chapter 10

I woke up late that Monday, and decided to investigate, i.e., harass the two guys who harassed poor Alyssa Arison. I started with Joe Cogan, the friendly neighborhood pot dealer. It was about a forty-five-minute ride to where he was in Souderton. I had asked Dan to access Cogan's phone so that I could know his exact whereabouts, and he was parked in the very same parking lot as the one at which poor Alyssa was murdered. There was the phone store, along with a pet supplies store, state store (to those of you from other areas, the state of Pennsylvania still sells us liquor if we want it), a Rite Aid, and a giant supermarket called appropriately enough Giant.

It was twelve-thirty on a cold, cloudy December afternoon. I had eaten raisin bran and drank a half-pot of coffee for breakfast, so I knew this would be a regular day. Dan said that Cogan was in the Giant, so I just parked my car in the lot between the two supermarket entrances (or exits, depending on your philosophical point of view), and waited. I did my business (numbers one and two) before leaving my place, so I was okay waiting for a while if need be. Hey, one must think of these things, especially before any kind of stakeout.

At twelve forty-nine, there he was, wheeling one of the junior carts with three bags of groceries in it. Cogan was short and thin, with wavy blonde hair, looked his mid-twenties age, and had the general vacant, vapid countenance of the habitual stoner. Because I am a Neanderthal, using Rachel's expression, I immediately sized him up as someone I could thrash around quite easily if the occasion called for it. This was a busy parking lot, so I couldn't go hog wild on the young man lest I be arrested by the same Souderton police force investigating Alyssa's murder.

As you would expect, after loading the bags in his trunk, the little shit did not wheel the cart to a cart receptacle, but just left it in the lot, thus blocking access to four parking spaces. The little shit deserved to be throttled just for that. He was driving a white Toyota sedan, which was spotless, I must admit. I guess the friendly neighborhood weed dealer needed to keep up appearances.

He hit the key fob and unlocked his driver's side door, and then I appeared seemingly from out of nowhere. Cogan was too mellow to look very alarmed, but he was put off. "Who the fuck are you, man?" See?

"Cogan, I know you want to get back home to put your shit away, but don't worry, it's cold out, your stuff will keep." I said this with a nice smile, like a neighbor introducing himself. I was twice his size which is always nice, so I was immediately placed in the alpha role. "I just want to ask you about Alyssa Arison." Again, with a bright smile for all of the shoppers to see.

"Fuck you. I already talked to the cops. Buzz off, old man."

Gosh darn it, I tried to be polite, but he went and got all rude. Silly rabbit. I hit him, hard, with a punch to his left kidney, which was covert enough not to be seen by the crowd, but effective enough to bring him to his knees. I just hoped that the patrons, most of whom were even older than me at that time of day, did not think that he was giving me a blowjob or anything. Not that there's anything wrong with that, I'm no homophobe, I'm just saying.

When Cogan caught his breath and stood up, he tried to look tough, but gave that approach up quickly when he recognized, as all of us Neanderthal men do, that I could easily break him in two. "Look. We went out a couple times. No big deal. Yes, I had a hard time letting go. Hasn't that ever happened to you?"

He did not address me as "old man" this time, which was gratifying. And Lord knows, yes it has happened to me, in fact I have written entire books about it; read *Torment*, it's good. I was developing empathy for Cogan, never a good turn when you're trying to intimidate somebody. "So you continued to stalk her and harass her? Seriously, dude, what's wrong with you?" I knew exactly what was wrong with him— he was lovesick. I've had the same affliction.

He looked genuinely ashamed of himself. "I know, you're right. Have you seen her, though? She's gorgeous. And she was really sweet, and I thought we had made a connection. I was wrong. But I didn't kill Alyssa, I swear to God." He looked me dead in the eye when he said this, perhaps deifying me for a moment.

Just like with Kret, I believed him, but my innocence barometer has been on the fritz over the last few years. I could not be sure. But there was nothing I could do about it in the Giant parking lot with dozens of people around. I tried my best to make my countenance look as mean as I could, but after his love confession, my heart wasn't in it. "Listen, Joe. Marijuana, rightly or wrongly, isn't legal here yet. I know cops all over the fucking place. I could make your life very difficult if I want to. I'm going to continue my investigation because Alyssa deserves it. Keep your nose clean."

I thought that was a nice little speech even though not a word of it was true. Then Cogan surprised me. "You're right. She does deserve it. She was the best girl I ever met. Nail the motherfucker who did it." At which point, I was tempted to hug the little pusher, but I just gave him a Clint Eastwood nod and headed to my car, which was parked about fifty yards away. Poor little punk.

Feeling all macho and punky myself, I decided to pay Steven Harrell a visit. I texted Dan to find his whereabouts, and he was at the dealership in Lansdale, where he worked. It was about a twenty-minute drive down Route 309, with surprisingly heavy traffic for a Monday afternoon, but not too bad. I was wearing my old winter coat, jeans, and sneakers, my usual winter uniform, but looking not so disheveled that I would walk onto the lot feeling self-conscious. The dealership was just south of the Montgomery Mall on 309, and I pulled onto the lot with my stomach already tightening in fear of a nest of salesmen preying upon me.

The place was replete with that erotic new car smell, but I did not let that deter my resolve. I didn't have to look around for a salesman, there he was right at the front door as I approached.

"Come on in, sir, come on in. My name is Steven Harrell. How can I help you today?" Not asking my name because like all salespeople, this was all about him.

"Um, I guess I wanted to take a look at a new Malibu."

"Excellent choice, sir. That's what I drive (as I knew), and it's been our most popular number." Number? "Can I take you to my desk and ask you a couple of questions, Mr.—"

"Lee. Dan Lee."

"Mr. Lee, I—"

"Did you say your name is Steven?" He nodded and was about to interject again. "I'm on a late lunch break from work." It was about one. I hadn't eaten lunch, and I was starting to feel it. "Would it be possible just to take a quick test drive, and you can tell me all about the car as we go? Maybe over the weekend, I can fill out whatever paperwork you might need."

Not one to let a prospect out the door on a technicality, he said, "Sure, Mr. Lee—"

"Dan, please."

"Dan, that's fine. Let me grab a set of keys from the office and I'll meet you right here." Off he shuffled (not a racist crack, he literally shuffled off to a back room somewhere), and out he came with keys in hand and wearing a sharp black overcoat. "It's a little nippy today."

As I followed Harrell onto the lot, I caught a whiff of his musky, expensive-smelling cologne. He was a tall, good-looking, well put-together guy. I say all this not out of latent homosexuality, but he didn't seem the type to pine over some girl, no matter how cute Alyssa was. We all know the young chicks love the BBC.

We walked over to the row of cars, and a dark blue Malibu with multiple stickers on the windows made a beep as he unlocked the door with his key fob. He opened the driver's side door for me like a true gentleman (I'm not a homo, shut up). "Make yourself comfortable, Dan. Roll that seat back if you need more room." Which I did as Harrell shuffled (you had to see it) around the front of the car to get in on the passenger's side. "Crank that heat up if you like, Dan, it's a little nippy today." Who the fuck talks like that?

I turned the heat on low and started to pull out of the lot. Harrell started to direct me which way to go on what I assumed was his usual planned route when I interrupted. "Steven, I know this area really well. Do you mind if I just drive? I promise to have you back to the dealership in less than fifteen minutes."

I could tell he was about to object, but then he thought better of it. "Sure, Phil. I could get in trouble for this. Not to mention for not checking your driver's license first. But I get that you're in a rush, and you look like a trustworthy fellow." Meaning that I was white and middle-aged. So, I used my elderly white man privilege.

Indeed, I did know Lansdale well, and I knew just where to take him. I made a sharp right on Hancock Road, the first intersection south of the dealership, drove about a quarter mile, and pulled onto an abandoned construction site. Harrell seemed ready to pitch the virtues of the Malibu when he said, "Um, Dan, are you okay? Why are we stopping here?"

Helpless elderly man act was over. I turned off the ignition. I gave him my best Charles Bronson (look him up, kids) glare and said, "Tell me about Alyssa Arison."

All color left his face. Okay, not all color, but you get my drift, so don't send me angry tweets. "I beg your pardon?"

"Steven, don't beg me yet, but if you don't answer my fucking question, you're going to be begging me to let you breathe. You have five seconds to tell me about Alyssa Arison."

Harrell wasn't a punk like Cogan, and he looked like he could take care of himself. Just his air, not his race, gave that impression. He did not want to acquiesce to my threat. But he let me off the lot without checking me out first in a brand new thirty-thousand-dollar car. He'd be fired for sure if we got into a fight. He knew it and I knew it. "She's just some girl I dated. Are you her daddy or something?"

More Bronson. "Steven, only one of us asks the questions, are we clear? What happened to Alyssa?"

Harrell's eyes darted all around, looking for a way out of this quagmire, but he could not find one. "I don't know. She ghosted me. And then I heard she died."

"Was murdered."

"Right."

"Why did you keep texting her and bothering her?"

All this time, Harrell was giving me his best Sidney Poitier (look him up too, kids) they call me Mr. Tibbs defiant stare, but his eyes lowered. "Look, I fell in love with her. What can I say? It was one way. But I kept at it, hoping to change her mind."

"You know men have been known to hurt women who wouldn't change their minds. Have you heard of O.J. Simpson, Harrell?"

Mr. Tibbs returned. "Oh, is this a race thing?"

"No. Neither was the O.J. arrest, so give it a rest." I love my puns.

"If you are suggesting I hurt Alyssa, you give it a

rest." This cat had claws. "I went over all this with the police. I've never committed a crime in my life. Look it up." Of course, I had, with the real Dan Lee's help. "I have no trouble meeting women." I believed him. "But Alyssa just got to me. Haven't you ever been in love when it didn't make sense?"

Oh yes. I looked at Harrell. My guilt barometer also told me that he was telling the truth. But maybe my barometer needed a tune up. I wasn't going to jostle Harrell around the way I did Cogan. A) Because he seemed like a nicer guy. And B) I didn't need some passerby to video me beating up a black man and have a TV crew standing outside my apartment building. C) I believed him, and a couple of kidney punches likely was not going to change that. D) I did not not fight him out of fear. He might be half my age, in better shape, but like I told Rachel, the Neanderthal man in me knew whose ass I could kick and whose I could not. I had zero fear of Steven Harrell. Just saying.

I switched from Bronson to Eastwood and gave him my best Clint nod. "Okay, Steven. I promised to have you back to the dealership in fifteen minutes. I'm a man of my word. Obviously, my name is not Dan Lee. If you try to find out who I am by my license plate and I get a knock on my door, either from the cops or some bad brothers you may know, I promise I will hurt you. Are we clear?"

"Sure. So, you're not a cop?"

I turned the ignition on. "No. I'm a private white dick. A PWD." He actually chuckled. "I'm just trying to find out who murdered Alyssa." I took a circuitous route, but we were approaching McCabe's.

"I hope you find him. Whatever your name is. And

no, I won't have it looked up." Harrell directed me to park the car by the side of the building. "Leave the motor on. I'll take care of it."

I scooted (a white man's shuffle) back to my own Chevy and drove home knowing that the knock on the door would never come. I liked Harrell. That didn't mean I wouldn't nail him if I found out he was the killer. I'm an equal rights man as you can tell.

****

Meanwhile, my erstwhile girlfriend had not called or texted while she was hobnobbing in Manhattan. Meaning my erstwhile book deal was in limbo.

But I kept on writing. This was my shot. When Bruce Springsteen went into a New York City studio to record the *Born To Run* album, that was his shot. After his first two albums failed miserably commercially, this album was indeed his last chance at stardom. If he failed, his record contract would likely have been canceled and he would have been put on the bus with a one-way ticket back to New Jersey.

When Sylvester Stallone, my Philly homeboy, wrote *Rocky* and demanded that he star in the movie, he knew that was his one shot at the big time, mirroring the fate of his famous fighting character. Both guys took their shots, hit nothing but net, and have been a part of the American Zeitgeist for almost fifty years.

But Bruce and Sly were under thirty. I was nearly twice that. This was not only my one shot, it was my last shot. I had to write a great book, and I had to mend fences with Rachel, or it was a one-way ticket to Palookaville for yours truly.

Writing. If you look at the backgrounds of most successful novelists, they came from wealthy, supportive families. They went to the best schools and were nurtured by caring teachers and sycophants. Their fates were practically pre-ordained.

Your humble narrator was born and raised in relative poverty. Going to a city public high school, barely graduating, never to step foot on a university campus. I was a cop, for Chrissakes, then a private dick. I had no business even attempting this late grasp for greatness. Before my late twenties, I never read a book; it was not part of how boys from my circumstances entertained themselves.

But I began to read. And dream. And think that these authors whom I was reading weren't so tough, I could step into the ring with most of them and hold my own. So, I wrote my little narratives, stumbled across a publishing executive from my high school days on Facebook, and then did what I had to do to fulfill my dream. But my advocate had to advocate for me, and my work had to be worthy of her advocation. So that weekend, I put my nose to the grindstone and worked at it. Waiting to hear from my would-be benefactor.

The plot of my case, however, had hit a standstill. Kret, Cogan, and Harrell all seemed genuinely innocent of murdering Alyssa Arison. She likely had plenty of unrequited admirers in and out of her life and the phone store every day. Any one of them could have pulled the trigger. Murders occur literally every day in this area. She could have been mistaken for someone else in the dark parking lot. Or just a random target of some deranged, drug-addled psycho.

Rachel was probably breezing through executive meetings, sashaying across expensive parties given by Manhattan's elite, never even giving a second thought to her recent abductor. Talk about ingratitude. It was getting difficult to motivate myself to write. If Rachel broke our saliva-moistened handshake agreement, what was the point? I'd be back to self-publishing and wracking up sales in the double digits. Effectively making my efforts at composition the equivalent of masturbation. What a mess.

I don't do drugs and rarely drink (so what was I doing trying to be a writer?), and I did neither that week, though I was feeling good and sorry for myself. Another form of masturbation.

Finally, a text from Rachel that Thursday night. — *Sorry I've been out of pocket. I have good news. Talk to you later in the week.*—

Hope, also like masturbation, springs eternal.

****

And so with the holidays and new year approaching, I had reason to smile. Maybe. I had no idea what Rachel's news could be, but just the fact that she was communicating with me again made me happy and pushed me back to my laptop to continue writing. Now that my investigation had ostensibly failed, it gave me something to do.

It's easy for a writer or anyone to be sarcastic. People are self-absorbed assholes. Yes, the world is a shithole, correct, and these things are fodder for ridicule, absolutely. There are "comedy" writers who do this, and they make sure to throw in gross amounts of sex and weed as they mock away at everything and everybody.

It's easy for a writer to create a protagonist who is just gosh-darned good. Help you across the street, lady? Can I help push your car out of the snow, buddy? Want me to sacrifice all of my time and money and dignity to assist you with your selfish goals? Why, I'd be glad to! People seem to like these books, or at least the publishing companies do, and they pump out books of these everyday martyrs to crowd the bookshelves and jam the websites to the exclusion of most everything else. The days of Jim Thompson and Mickey Spillane were over. In a world of senseless greed, violence, and cheating, these heroes gave us hope. At least fictionally.

But I kept at it, trying to thread the needle between sentimentality and cynicism, with the faith that people would like it. Or at least one person who was on her way back to Philadelphia from Manhattan would like it. These paragraphs weren't going to write themselves, as I kept telling myself.

****

Rachel called me that night and asked me if I'd like to visit over the weekend. "Yes," I said. Which didn't help with my word count.

The rest of the week was a blur as I didn't talk to or see anybody, which wasn't unusual for me. I went to the gym a few times, hit the supermarket, but that was it. I wasn't nervous about seeing Rachel, but I was excited. Because I had nothing else to do and no one else to see.

I yanked a ten-year-old shirt and a twenty-year-old sweater out of the back of my closet, along with the only pair of jeans that was comfortable for my middle-aged waistline, and my sneakers because I didn't want to seem like I gave my courtin' outfit much thought.

I arrived at Rachel's at two. It was a cold Saturday afternoon with light flurries, and I drove instead of taking public transportation, which runs about once every lunar eclipse on weekends. I pulled into a parking lot on Ludlow, which would cost me more than my entire outfit did, and walked the couple of blocks to Rachel's intimidating building. I did not bring wine or flowers, because I was trying to play it cool while my heart was beating louder than a big bass drum. That's not plagiarism, it's homage, Mick.

After I made it through the deep cavity check at the building's security desk, I took the elevator on up, knocked on the door, and Ms. Arison was looking mighty fine in a form-fitting deep blue dress. She rushed over to kiss me on the cheek (yay!) and took my coat, looking at it like someone had defecated in her hands.

"It's good to see you, Phil. Sorry to have been aloof, but I had some personal things to take care of as well as some work issues." She sounded genuinely apologetic, but did not look it. However, I was not one to quibble.

"It's fine, I had stuff to do too." I had gone to the bathroom over fifty times, for instance. Rachel invited me to sit on her couch, and she sat to my right. Which I hate, because I always feel like my left is my better profile, but I did not want to seem vain. We chitchatted about politics, movies, whatever, and I finally asked her about her good news.

"I've gotten your book on the fast track, Phil! Green lights all the way. As soon as you're finished with it, our top fiction editor will work with you on honing it, and then unless it's terrible, which I know it won't be, Marketing will get it out there to libraries, the few remaining brick and mortar bookstores, and of course will promote it heavily on the important online platforms!" She seemed pleased with herself, and I was pleased with her too.

"That is awesome, Rachel. Thank you. I am trying, really hard, to make this my best book ever. I'd like to dedicate the novel to you, if that's all right."

She pondered that for a moment, and said, "Thank you, Phil, I would be honored. Perhaps just use my initials, though, so it won't seem like I had undue influence in getting it published."

"Is kidnapping you and holding you hostage considered undue influence?"

She shook her head as if to say, what a fucking asshole, which was spot on. "Let's not ruin the moment, shall we?"

And so, I did not. Rachel used one of her phone apps to order a complete sushi dinner for us (I still used cardboard menus to order pizza when I ordered in), and then things turned romantic. This is when the camera pans from the couch to the window, at least in movies made before 1970. Now, of course, if we don't see the beads of sweat on a woman's boobs, it gets a G-rating.

I slept over, and Rachel had already made a pot of coffee while I was still sleeping. I checked my phone as I ambled toward the bathroom for my pre-breakfast pee when I opened a text from Dan Lee.

—*Just thought you might want to know. Andrea Goldsmith is dead.*—

Hey now. For those of you with scorecards, that's Andrea Goldsmith, ex-wife of one Stanley Kret, the ex-husband of one Rachel Arison. That's a 4-6-3 double-play.

I was fast asleep when the towers were shattered on 9/11. Because I like to sleep late. So I can't say that I suspected something fishy after the first tower came crumbling down and knew that it was nefarious when the second one did. I woke up a couple hours after the whole she-bang, and saw it reported as a terrorist attack at about eleven o'clock on that horrible Tuesday morning.

As a detective, I am supposed to have good deductive reasoning, but I don't know if mine is better than most people's; probably not. I graduated in the bottom half of my high school class lest you forget.

But it doesn't take a genius or a math wizard to know that one and one make two, baby. Alyssa Arison, secret crush of Stanley Kret was murdered. And Andrea Goldsmith, the second, younger wife of the chubby schlub, was dead now too. I didn't know the circumstances. Maybe she got hit by a falling tree or had a stroke. People die from all kinds of things at all kinds of ages these days.

I took a hard look at my book benefactor. She was sitting in her exquisite dining room drinking what I imagined was exquisite coffee. Already dressed, albeit casually, and ready to meet the world. And her publishing protégé.

My pre-coffee mind is even more sluggish than my post-coffee one, but I quickly did the calculations in my head. Alyssa Arison was murdered just before I brought Rachel in as my houseguest. Andrea Goldsmith died while my cute coffeemaker was up in New York. Ergo, fuck. Was the woman about to make me a big-time author also a murderer? I had to find out from Dan, quickly, about the circumstances of Andrea's death. But Rachel smiled her pretty smile and said, "Good morning, sunshine!"

This accomplished, lovely woman was about to make my dreams come true, and give my heretofore meaningless life meaning. Okay, not completely meaningless. Sorry, Jessica and Anna. I didn't have time to text a reply to Dan. So, I just said, "Good morning." That's what you call deep improv skills.

"You sure sleep late, don't you, Phil?" I glanced at my phone, which felt like a hand grenade with explosive information, and saw that it was 9:54.

"Is that late for a Sunday?"

"The morning is half over, sleepyhead." She got up from her exquisite chair and gave me a quick kiss on the mouth, politely ignoring my morning breath. "It's a beautiful day outside. Do you want to walk around South Street?" Philadelphia's decaying answer to Greenwich Village.

I didn't know what to do. But I wanted to get out of there, talk to Dan, and figure out my next move. "Hey. I have some stuff to do, cases to do paperwork on and all. I'm sorry, Rachel. I didn't expect to stay the night. I should get back."

A cloud of disappointment and anger crossed her pretty blonde brow, like they say in old literature, but she recovered quickly. "I understand. I was away all week to do my thing. So, whether you have actual work to do or not, you're reacting like any man would."

"It's not like that. I swear—"

"It's okay." She kissed me again and stepped out of the way so I could get at the coffee machine, like a heroin addict for the needle. I drank four cups of her exquisite coffee, tried to appear nonchalant, and put my Saturday clothes back on, no shower or tooth brushing necessary. I made with the light yakety-yak and wanted to excuse myself gallantly from her apartment. Then she asked, "Has your friend planted incriminating evidence on Stan's phone and computer yet?"

Shit. No, he had not, because I told him to hold off. How to broach this subject without setting off the timebomb. "Uh, he had some issues doing it. I should have told you sooner. He, uh, said Kret had firewalls which made planting things on his devices more difficult than he had anticipated." Sounds plausible, right?

The dark cloud passed again. "I am disappointed, Phil. But I understand. He is working on it, though?"

"Um, yes, diligently. Dan really is the best, so if he says he will get it done, he will. Just a temporary glitch is what he called it."

"All right, Phil." I knew that she was angry, but there really was nothing more to say on the subject. I excused myself politely from her apartment.

As soon as I was on the elevator, I texted Dan.

—WTF?! How did she die?—

Dan was either busy or busy being a dick, and he didn't text me back until I retrieved my car (sixty-eight dollars!) from the lot and headed toward the Sure-Kill Expressway. Before I reached the on-ramp, he finally replied. I read it at the traffic light.

—I don't know. I have a program that directs me to names that I had recently looked up. I designed it myself. I got a link to an obituary in the New York Daily News saying that Andrea Goldsmith, forty-three, legal secretary, had died last Monday. And the usual remembrances by her loved ones. I tried to find the cause, but I haven't been able to. I'm sorry. Likely natural causes or I likely would have seen otherwise.—

I could not bring myself to say more, or to thank him. I just got on the highway, mostly devoid of traffic on a Sunday morning heading out of Center City, and drove straight home. I made myself a thick peanut butter sandwich (Jif chunky always), washed it down with one percent milk straight from the gallon jug, and crashed in my bedroom. I mean, I had only gotten nine hours sleep.

By the time I got home, Dan had taken it upon himself to investigate further. However, unlike his usual homeruns, he swung and missed. I hadn't looked at my phone while driving (and no one should: public service announcement), and waited until after my lunch, but he had texted:

—No sign of foul play. No autopsy. Best I could come up with is that she died of brain trauma, seemingly from a fall in her apartment. It happens.—

So, it might have been a coincidence that Andrea Goldsmith died while Rachel was in town. Probably the likely scenario. Why investigate it further? Why confront her? She was my almost girlfriend. More importantly, she was my almost publisher. Why risk all that? Why alienate her? For some wild supposition?

I texted Dan, thanked him in reply, and told him what I had told Rachel about a glitch preventing him from incriminating Kret with kiddie porn, and he replied with the thumbs up emoji.

Meanwhile, as long as I could keep Rachel on my side, I was on my way. My one shot to almost fame and almost fortune. Nobody was paying me to be a detective, and nobody seemed to be questioning Goldsmith's death. People die. Naturally, freakishly, it happens. I wanted my book out, and I wanted to be on the Today show. But first…I had to finish it.

Part Two

Chapter 12

"You know, the only shades of grey in modern fiction come in blocks of fifty." You can't repeat a good line often enough.

This was me on a radio interview with Philly's public radio station, XPN. I had no agent, so Bryce Douglas's Marketing team had arranged a bunch of interviews for me, loading up on my hometown's local media to build the Philly market. My novel was about to be released, so this was called priming the pump.

"How do you come up with your ideas, Phil? Is this novel autobiographical?" This was the smooth-voiced radio lady asking what I imagined was her list of prepared questions. It was barely after seven in the morning, but luckily, I was able to do my side of the interview from home on my laptop, so I didn't have to wake up too crazy early.

"It's not unlike what I imagine an actor does, Renee." I was obviously feeling myself now, pontificating not only about writing, but acting too. "You take people and elements from your own life and create a new character. But that's what it is. A character. It's not me, and the things that happen in the book did not happen to me."

"You didn't kidnap anyone to get a publishing deal?" She laughed.

So did I. "No, nothing like that. One of the higher-ups at Bryce Douglas and I went to high school together. So yes, I had an 'in', and I waxed poetic about that in my novel. But Bryce's publishers and editors still had to give their approval, and I like to think that I earned it." Did that sound defensive?

"Yes, I found your novel fascinating. After writing nine that were published by smaller companies, what's it been like working with a large, established firm like Bryce Douglas?"

"Professional. That's the word that I would use." Oh, I was better at bullshitting than I ever imagined. "Everything that they do is professional, and I could not be more pleased with how my novel, *The Last Shot* has been handled by Bryce. And with how I have been treated."

She laughed again. "Good job, Phil. Always get the title out to the public! The book is coming out next month, just in time for Father's Day. Coincidence?" This interview was on the first Wednesday of the following May; the book was getting published at lightning speed from what Rachel told me, hitting the streets and the websites less than six months after I had finished the manuscript.

"I don't know. I leave all that up to the Marketing folks. I don't perceive that *The Last Shot* is necessarily a 'male' novel, but I imagine their demographics experts wanted to get the book out in time for Memorial Day and Father's Day. That's *The Last Shot* at stores and online on May twenty-fourth."

Renee laughed again. Nothing delights a jokester more than a receptive audience. "Nicely done, Phil." Somebody must have said something to her that I couldn't hear because she said, "Thank you for speaking with us today, Phil. Now let's take a look at today's weather." And I was off the call.

Everything was going as per my plan.

Rachel had done it. She had gotten me the book deal. She got Marketing behind me. This radio interview was my thirtieth or so in the past few weeks, and I had at least that many more already lined up. Radio, Podcasts, Internet, book clubs, television, and all the rest. And all from the comfort of my home. I didn't have to schlep around to all these studios and places and God knows what else. I was Mr. Zoom and Mr. Teams, meeting with people the new-fashioned way. Virtually.

Rachel and I were still seeing each other, but I wouldn't call her my girlfriend. I finally gave Dan the go-ahead to release the Kraken by putting illicit porn on Kret's devices. Kret had been duly arrested and was out on bail awaiting trial later in the year.

And Bryce Douglas was in fact priming the pump, getting my book out there to bookstores and libraries, and featuring it and me on as many prominent book sites as one could imagine. My backstory was *the* story. How a real life middle-aged private detective, who'd been published and self-published unsuccessfully, was now the book world's darling boy. Like Don King used to say: Only in America.

But it wasn't only in America. I was rockin' all over the world. Being glib with interviewers across the globe. They all found me charming! *Me*! What used to be thought of as misanthropic (book title idea: Miss Ann Thropic) was now considered crusty good fun. My sarcastic jibes at other writers were considered the height of hilarity (book title idea: The Height of Hilarity). I wasn't J.K. Rowling or James Patterson or Stephen King, but Bryce placed me at a rung just below, and announced that my other nine novels would also be released by the end of May. Hollywood showed interest in several of my novels, and in me personally!

It was thought that my life would make an interesting biopic. Working class loser becomes semi-famous detective becomes almost famous author. Everybody likes an underdog story, as I was told by Rachel and her Bryce minions. I was Rocky for the new millennium. I had scores of well-known writers and actors inquiring about writing the screenplay and maybe even playing me.

My pretty face was all over the place. I'd even been asked for autographs when I food shopped at the Giant or filled up my gas tank. Bryce gave me a fifty-thousand-dollar advance and apologized to me because it was so small. "We're really sorry, Phil. You are a new author with us, so we have to be prudent. But you should have ten times that by this time next year." I grudgingly accepted their draconian terms.

Rachel and I had become close. Again, not officially boyfriend and girlfriend, but we saw enough of each other and slept together frequently enough to make our relationship everything but. Now that I could have gotten hot groupies, I remained true to my benefactor, publisher, recent hostage, and possible murderer. I'm old-fashioned that way.

I tried to remain humble and lovable like Underdog. I kept my crappy car. I kept my crappy apartment. I did not keep my crappy furniture, and treated myself to all new stuff, and some new, sharp duds to boot. Including two boots. It's puns like that which have made me a literary star.

My children, not surprisingly, did not treat me any differently, and for that I was both grateful and a little pissed off. Did John Grisham's kids give him grief? Probably so.

I knew what intense fame could do to people. I would never be that intensely famous, but having a cult following is still a following. I would aim to keep my head and keep most of my money. I had never been successful before, but I enjoyed the feeling.

****

Things were still cooking with Lady Rachel, and I think she got a genuine kick of working with me during the embryonic process of TLS (my abbreviation for *The Last Shot,* which I may use henceforth), seeing it through the final version, and now getting it out into the public. Writing a book is not completely unlike having a child. It usually takes about nine months (at least for me), you take care during the gestation period not to hurt your baby, and then you push it out with the pain and anxiety of knowing that once it's out, it's out, and there's no going back. I can hear literally every female reader telling me to go fuck myself, that the two have nothing in common, to which I say, you might be right. But, I still like the metaphor. Maybe this book was like that for the childless Rachel.

I hadn't mentioned Andrea Goldsmith's death, and I had no idea if Rachel knew about it. I had to assume and hope not, or at least hope that she wasn't a murderer because that would present a real moral quandary.

Rachel had gone where few women had gone

before; she had visited my apartment, which she initially called "quaint", and then referred to it as "freshman dorm." I had not gone to college, but I had two daughters who had; they are girls, however, and their aesthetic standards are higher than mine.

This was before I got the advance check, and yes, her comments prompted me to get new furniture, but not a new address. Rachel then referred to my apartment as "grad student dorm," which I took as a compliment.

She came over on a Sunday, the first day in May to strategize before most of the Marketing was executed, and to "cuddle". She was wearing a designer t-shirt and jeans, the kind of look that says, "I'm comfortable in your low class racially diverse neighborhood," even though her outfit probably cost more than any suit I owned.

"You know, Phil, I would have been more than happy to help you shop for furniture." Her passive-aggressive way of saying that my choices were shit. "But this is a man's apartment, and I suppose it should represent the man who lives here." Her passive-aggressive way of saying that I too was shit. I don't know, I got a living room set in brown faux leather from a chain store that offered the worst in customer service. I don't want to name names or get sued. But it was Bob's Discount Furniture. Just saying.

"If your book is to be released in three weeks, we have to really push, Phil. Marketing will get the word out on the book nerd sites, but I want a broader audience for you. I don't know how you've published books without a website. I already hired a web development company that I've worked with in

Manhattan, and your site should go live in a couple of days. People will want to find you, reach out to you, learn your story as much as your books' stories. I need you to write a five-hundred-word autobiography, and another at one hundred words. The lengthier one will be on your website, and the shorter one we'll post on the Bryce Douglas site as well as on the various book nerd platforms and your book cover jackets. All of which is designed to maximize your SEO, of course."

"Okay." My passive-passive way of saying that I had no clue about these things, and I was leaving these adult things to Mommy. Rachel had not shown this kink in the bedroom, but she manifested it in every other area of our relationship.

"I have also set up an appointment for you tomorrow with a local photographer that Bryce has used in the past. For your website, press releases, and of course, your book's back cover." Rachel then gave me a business card for the photographer. By local, she meant a block from her apartment, but a three-hour round-trip for yours truly. "I would pack a bag with a few different looks. Casual Phil, tough guy Phil, sensitive author Phil, professional Phil. At the very least, wear a shirt and tie to her place, and pack a couple of casual short sleeve shirts. Let the women out there, and men for that matter, see those rippling biceps. You'll have the women swooning and the men feeling an affinity with your Neanderthal side."

"Okay."

"Our staff has edited your other nine books by removing your many typos and tightening up the prose."

"Shouldn't I have some say as to what they can

edit and what they can't?"

"Under normal conditions we allow that, but to get your books market ready quickly, we are skipping this step. These are the best editors in the world, Phil. Your books will be that much better for their pruning. And before you express any indignation, think of how many copies your books sold when you were the primary editor. Plus, you gave us the right to edit your work in the contract that you signed." Which, lazy and trusting fuck that I am, I had never read.

Having other people changing, adding, or trimming my books without my consent made me angry. It would be like changing aspects of my children without my say-so. "I don't know if I feel comf—"

"Dude, it's in the contract that you gladly signed, so get over it." This was tough boss Rachel.

"Okay," I said, chastened.

"We are implementing your idea of combining two of your novellas for each of these releases. You have eight Phil Allman books, so naturally the first two are volume one, the second two are volume two, and so forth. We will have to release your hilarious yet pointed satire (her words) *The Last Man On Earth* separately, however. As I told you when I first read it, the first two-thirds are excellent and good to go, but we had to clean things up a little bit at the end. And then naturally, your new novel will be published as a standalone. We have had to work at breakneck speed to get these out before Memorial Day weekend and Father's Day, and I had to use the whip hand on the staff to get it done."

"Okay."

"We are marketing you and your books nationwide and worldwide, but I want to play up your Philadelphia roots and really hit the local market hard. Our goal is to make you the most successful mystery author ever out of Philadelphia. So, expect to do a lot of local interviews, public appearances, and readings from your book over the next six weeks. All virtually. Pre-release publicity and post-release publicity. I will prepare you and coach you what to say. But always be yourself."

I was in no position to argue. "Okay."

"Meaning, none of your smart-ass politically incorrect banter. We don't want one of your jokes to be taken out of context and used to stifle your success before it even starts. I understand your dry sense of humor, and it will play well with the media, but keep it clean and keep it woke. We have a few dozen interviews already lined up, all of which you can do from home."

"Okay."

"Great. Let's have sex first, and then we'll get to work."

****

So, I was My Fair Lady, the working-class non-hero getting prepared to speak with journalists, web bloggers, book nerds, Podcast douchebags, and the like. I was being transformed into an urbane, articulate sophisticate. "But isn't part of my story rags to potential riches? Shouldn't I be myself? Look at Mickey Spillane. He sold millions of books in large part because he looked and sounded like a punk from the streets."

Rachel listened to my plea, then turned into Mommy. "Who's the publishing executive here, Phil? When was Mickey Spillane popular? Before either of us was born. Today's fiction book audience consists almost entirely of college educated people, mostly women. They don't listen to these Podcasts to hear street talk. They want to hear George Clooney. Someone funny, well-spoken, and self-deprecating. And you can be that person. Just pronounce your words fully and slowly, and no f-bombs."

"The rain in Spain stays mainly in the plain."

"By George, I think he's got it." At which point she gave me a kiss in much the same way you give your dog a treat for not crapping on the furniture.

****

And so, the interviews continued, as did the same inane questions and robotic answers.

"Phil, was it frustrating before your deal with Bryce reaching such a small audience?"

"Writing without an audience is akin to masturbation. You're just doing it to satisfy yourself."

"Marci, your very young wife. Er, ex-wife. How much of her character is fictional?"

"I appreciate the question. I will not comment on the validity of my characters or situations. It's up to individual readers as to what they believe."

"Well, we know for a fact that you are friends with New Jersey rock legend Felix Brigati. What's he really like?"

"Exactly what you probably think. Committed. Dedicated. Talented. Narcissistic."

These were repeated dozens of times, almost verbatim, but the trick is to act like you're hearing the questions for the first time. "Is it better to be rich and famous or poor and anonymous?" You want to say, "Take a fucking wild guess." But you don't.

"Anonymity is good for a writer. It enables the

author to observe people without being observed in turn. And poverty keeps you hungry to try your best."

Real answer? "Being poor and anonymous is like death in America. Nobody wants to know you, see you, or hear from you. You're irrelevant and made to feel that way every bloody second of your life." Instead, you quip, "Though being rich and famous has its perks." You wink, they chuckle, and your humility is applauded. It's all bullshit.

****

Shortly before the official release of TLS, the Bryce team somehow got me a one-on-one interview with Mary Emerick, perhaps America's most noted literature columnist with one of New York's, and therefore the world's most prestigious monthly magazines. I knew almost nothing about the literary world, yet even I had heard of Ms. Emerick.

The interview was initially to take place at the magazine's offices in Midtown Manhattan on the third Monday in May at four o'clock. Rachel had work to do in Philly, but she wished me luck on my trip and the interview. "This is an incredible opportunity, Phil. Her articles hit publications and websites all over the world, which very important people read. Some of my most veteran authors would kill for a chance to interview with Mary. I would love to go with you, but I am so swamped with work and meetings, I just can't. I'm sure you will do fine, though. Don't be nervous. It will be a long day. If you want to stay over, Bryce will cover your expenses, and I suggest that you use that perk." Rachel being the Good Mommy.

I packed an overnight bag and, not wanting to tax myself too much, I booked a relatively inexpensive room at a hotel very close to Penn Station. For you puzzle fans out there, both the hotel and the magazine have the same name, so figure it out.

I drove up to Trenton, parked my car at a lot near the train station, and took Amtrak, not cheapo New Jersey Transit up to New York, all of this on Bryce's dime. I was movin' on up. To the Upper West Side.

It was a perfect spring day, sunny, nice breeze, temps in the sixties, and I wore an old sport jacket/blazer that I found in the back of my closet over a golf shirt (even though I have never played golf other than mini), jeans, and sneakers. I looked not unlike the mismatched furniture that had adorned my living room apartment until a few weeks ago.

I somehow find taking the train exciting, almost like going back in time a hundred years, and Amtrak's speed was probably akin to trains in the early twentieth century. But my appointment was at four, and having boarded the train at around noon, I was in no rush. I disembarked in the hectic, scary, huge Penn Station, right in the middle of Manhattan and adjacent to the famous Madison Square Garden where I had seen my first magical, majestic Felix Brigati concert some forty years prior, promoting his good but not great double album *The Ravine.*

I tried to get to my room at the hotel but seeing as how I arrived there over an hour before check-in, the best that I could do was leave my bag so I could be unencumbered to walk around the city. The magazine's offices were downtown, not far from Ground Zero, but Mary Emerick, in a last-minute switcheroo, was working from her apartment on the Upper West Side, so I just walked the couple of miles west on Broadway, the quickest way to get there on foot according to my GPS machine.

Walking around New York is like nothing else and nowhere else in the country or the world. I haven't been everywhere like Johnny Cash, but I had been around enough and listened to and read about folks who had traveled extensively, and this sentiment was universally embraced. During the day, you don't see the city's famous denizens of the night, but the mix and melding of races, classes, ages, languages spoken and yelled made me feel like I was in an outdoor U.N. building, and in some sense, I was. The streets were crowded with people meandering to and fro, but not crazy jammed like it was during the Christmas season, when I had taken the girls for day trips a couple of times. Nobody made eye contact, and now with cell phones and headsets, it was hard to distinguish people talking to themselves from people talking to someone else. The psychos and the businesspeople all shared the streets and avenues, and I found that invigorating.

High end shops and eateries were adjacent to low end shops and eateries, and it all seemed very democratic to me. The pretty girls were more numerous the further west I walked. I stopped in a coffee shop in the upper fifties because I had time to kill, and I required caffeine. I wanted to sound sharp for this lofty publication and not like some low-rent rube off the Philly streets.

After sitting at the counter for a couple of cups of coffee and a slice of cherry crumb pie (mmm!), I walked another mile or so to Ms. Emerick's lofty, swanky, intimidating apartment building on Seventh Avenue and around Seventieth, adjacent to Central

Park. Like Rachel's, the building had the uniformed doorman salaried to keep people like me from entering. The lobby had chandeliers, plush carpeting, expensive looking seating areas, and even a baby grand piano! I didn't know her sources of income, but I thought, man, these magazine writers sure do well. I stopped at the security desk, and the guard asked for my name, my driver's license to prove it, and he scanned a list, and said, "Twenty-third floor," sounding like a throaty Barry White.

After I exited the elevator, Emerick's apartment was one of only four on the entire floor, and hers was the second to the right. The security guy had announced me, and the door was ajar. I still knocked, and she approached the foyer. I had looked her up online, of course, but she was prettier in person. Jet black hair swirled above her clear blue eyes and classic features. She was wearing what I suppose you would call a business dress, which was a matching purple skirt and jacket over a white blouse and above violet pumps. She extended her hand, and I shook it quickly because I realized that mine was sweaty.

"Come in, Mr. Allman. I have been looking forward to meeting you." These weren't words I had heard frequently in my life, so I replied, "Me too," like a kid on his first day of third grade or a sexual assault victim. I wanted to take Rachel's advice and not be nervous, but between Emerick's beauty and her place, which looked like something from a 1930s Manhattan movie soap opera, I failed. Paintings and furniture and carpet and knickknacks that were all so beautiful and tasteful and out of my league that I was having trouble breathing.

And Mary Emerick added to my asthmatic state. I had learned that she was forty-one, was a Harvard grad from an elite family, and took to journalism as a way of slumming it. Her talent, love of books, and of course connections, got her to where she was. Which was three feet in front of me, and I was perspiring like Albert Brooks in Broadcast News. Look it up.

To her credit, she sensed my unease and said, "Please, sit down, Mr. Allman? Would you like a drink?"

I nodded yes to sitting down and said, "Water." Always the conversationalist. She left the room to go into what I assumed was the kitchen and returned with a bottle of Evian. I probably could have used something stronger, but I wanted to stay sharp for this interview. I gingerly sat on her white leather sofa, and she sat adjacent on the matching loveseat, her lovely legs crossed.

"Mr. Allman, I don't know CPR, so I hope you will calm down." It was funny, and I laughed, which broke the spell somewhat.

"I'm sorry, Ms. Emerick—"

"Mary."

"And I'm Phil. I am not used to all this, and I frankly feel out of my element."

Mary was not so obtuse as to not recognize the situation, so instead of saying I should not feel that way, she said, "Perfectly understandable. I'm the famous literary journalist here in her swanky Manhattan apartment, and I have the ability to make or break you." She smiled then. My pulse increased by about twenty beats per minute. "I promise I am not here to break you." I felt my pulse decrease by about fifteen beats per minute then. "I've read an advance copy of your new novel, and I like it. So, let's start there."

No matter what I or anyone says, every writer loves to talk about his or her work. "Thanks. I am aware that I'm not a literary lion, and my books don't compare with what you're used to reading."

"You're right, they don't." I must have appeared dumbstruck because I was, and she chuckled. "It's not what I'm used to reading. It's gritty. And real. And heartfelt. Most of all, it's funny. You don't aim to show me or anybody else how smart you are. And that's refreshing."

The ice having been shattered, the conversation became easy. After all, I was dating one of the leading publishing executives in the entire world (after kidnapping her, no less), so why should a conversation with a beautiful journalist writing about my book be all that difficult? We spoke for a few hours (the specifics of which I cannot share because they include spoilers), and before I knew it, it was dark outside. "Are you in town overnight, Phil?"

"Yes, I'm staying near Penn Station." I did not mention the hotel, because it was not exactly New York's finest.

"Do you have friends here? Dinner plans?"

I thought about saying something cute like "I do now," but I refrained. "No."

"Good." She speed-dialed somebody and made a reservation for two in about a half-hour. She mentioned the name of the restaurant, which I had surprisingly heard of. "It's terribly expensive, but it's quiet and the food is excellent. Don't worry, the magazine is paying for it."

And so, your favorite Philadelphia kidnapper and detective went out to dinner at one of the world's most famous and exclusive restaurants with the most formidable writer about books in America. And, oh yeah, ya boy did okay. And then some.

Chapter 13

As one who decries formulas, I know the most formulaic turn of events is the private dick getting laid by a woman of the upper crust. "Yeah, right," if not "yuck," come to mind when I read it. But what can I say? Facts are facts and your protagonist now had two highly successful, beautiful women in the publishing industry notched on his belt. Did I feel guilty about my bedding of Mary while Rachel was back in Philly? Hell no. I don't see any rings on my finger. We weren't even boyfriend and girlfriend. She was free to do whatever and whomever, and so was I. Wasn't I? Rachel might even applaud my efforts to get positive publicity for my books. After all, much of her reputation was on the line as it pertained to my success. Right?

Rachel did, though, have a jealous streak. At the very least. A murderously jealous streak, perhaps. As such, I judiciously decided not to mention the lurid details of my evening with Mary Emerick, other than to say that I thought the interview went well. Discretion being the better part of valor and all that. Mary, when alluding to Rachel, also confessed that she had once or twice dated Kret (!), a fact that absolutely blew my mind. "The poor man seemed to fall in love with me," Mary said. "I could not deal with his crudeness or brutishness for more than two dates." I did not give Rachel that morsel of information, either.

And Mary's article, when published online later that week, did wonders for me in terms of sales and prestige. She called me the "Avatar of Philly Noir", a nice, easy-to-remember rhyming title. "Allman's protagonist breaks the fourth wall by dishing the dirt on everyone and everything around him. He strips himself naked for the world to revile. Utterly unlike any fiction since Jim Thompson." Wow.

But Rachel was smarter and more intuitive than I. We met for dinner at a casual bistro on Chestnut Street a few evenings later. It was a perfect setting with perfect weather; we sat at a table outside and had a couple of drinks before eating. Guinness for me, white wine spritzer for Rachel. She was unusually chatty as we sipped our beverages. "Tell me all about your interview. I met Mary at a few functions when Stan and I were together, but I never really had a substantive conversation with her. How did it go?"

"Uh. Good."

"Were you nervous?"

"At first, but she, um, put me at ease."

"I've never been to their offices. Were they fully staffed, even in the aftermath of Covid?"

"Um. She, uh, her plans changed at the last minute and she had me go to her place. Her apartment, I mean."

"Oh. I know that in addition to her job, her family is fairly wealthy. Was it lavish?"

"Uh. No. I mean, yeah, compared to my place, yes. But compared to yours, not really." I forced a laugh.

"Well, her rent in Manhattan is probably three times mine as opposed to Philly. And I have had to earn my rent. My family never had much to give me."

"Yeah. Same with me." I wanted to change the subject. Quickly. "What happens when the book is actually published next week?"

"It's not exactly like a Hollywood premiere, Phil. But Bryce will make announcements on all the various book sites and focus on readers of mysteries and noir. People who buy books from similar contemporary authors."

"Most of whom I hate."

She leaned across the table and kissed me. "I know, baby. You're better than they are. And I think that your book sales will eventually prove it." She sipped more of her drink. "Do you think that Mary is pretty?"

Whoa, here was the proverbial loaded question. If I said no, she'd know I'm lying. If I said yes, she'd suspect something. I had to turn on that old Phil finesse. "Uh, I don't know. I guess. It was like a job interview; I didn't really think of her in that way." Not bad.

"Did you use the job interview trick of imagining her in her underwear?" Rachel then forced a laugh.

I did too. "Ha. No, I didn't think of it."

"Didn't you think that she was aloof? I found her to be an enigma."

"No, she's white." I then started laughing uncontrollably at my bad joke while Rachel alternatively rolled her eyes and shook her head.

"I hope that you didn't succumb to this lowbrow humor with Mary. What did you do for dinner?"

Another dangerous query. If she ever saw Mary, the subject of dinner could conceivably come up. But if I said that we dined together, this inquiry would turn into an inquisition. "I just ate at the diner adjacent to the hotel."

She nodded. "Okay, don't forget to turn in all your receipts. The trip is on Bryce."

Receipts! Damn. I just nodded, knowing that I'd been played. Well.

We continued having our supper as if nothing had just transpired. Before our entrees came, I excused myself to the restroom and texted Mary from one of the large, lavish stalls.

—*Nothing happened between us! Including dinner. Okay?*—

She did not reply until hours later with a thumbs-up emoji. I thought about texting back a J5 video of *Stop, The Love You Save May Be Your Own*, but I wasn't drunk enough to pull that off.

****

"What do you listen to?" This was a phone interview that I was doing that Thursday for a national music magazine and website, which Rachel felt was important so I could generate some younger readers, who she said were buying books now more than ever. "You allude to music very frequently in your novels. But it's almost always from artists and songs from over forty years ago." The interviewer's name was Traci Morgan, which I assumed was authentic and not an homage to the Walmart truck struck comedian.

Traci sounded very young and cute. Almost like my second wife. I didn't want to alienate her or their readers, but I wanted to be honest. "I listen to things from all genres and eras. Really. I have two daughters in their twenties who frequently recommend people for me to listen to. But"—I hesitated, knowing I was going to sound fossil-esque— "A lot of it is so...depressing. I listen to these people, and I can hear their cleverness and the honesty of their emotions, and I think that's great. But there's no sense of joy. Like even during the last year of his life, when Elvis was both morbidly obese and just plain morbid, there was still a sense of humor and a sense of 'life' there. Almost all of his songs were about painful lost love or death. And he threw off whatever fetters had been in place and allowed us to hear his pain. And see it in his live shows. But even at this stage, he would mix in humor. And shtick. Because he understood that it was a 'show'. That he was an entertainer. To stand onstage and be lifeless and morose the whole time doesn't interest me." I realized I was rambling like an old man telling this girl and her audience to get off his lawn. And she sounded like someone whom I would like to get off my lawn and into my house.

"Yeah, Phil. I hear you. But these are depressing times we're living in. And these musicians are simply reflecting that pain, which is why it resonates with so many young people."

"Times are no more depressing than they've ever been. I just feel like people, especially young people, are being encouraged to wallow in it." Fuck, I was alienating her, and I knew it.

"How about Marci?" Uh oh. Bringing up my teenage ex-wife in this context could not be good. "Did she share your music tastes and philosophies?"

"No. She had her own tastes, which veered toward the very music I just railed against. My Chemical Romance was her favorite. I don't impose my tastes on anyone, but you asked me my opinion, so I gave it." Sounding so defensive that I was making myself nauseous.

"Okay. Well, I think that I have enough for my piece. Thank you, Phil." And our conversation was over. I just hoped she wouldn't skewer me in her article. Not that I really cared, but Rachel would never let me hear the end of it.

****

"There is no such thing as bad publicity." We have all heard this from Hollywood and media types. Careers have been built on bad publicity. Kim Kardashian comes immediately to mind. But when you are the one on the receiving end of such publicity, it doesn't seem like a good thing. Traci Morgan's exposé hit the newsstands and the world wide web on the weekend before TLS was released. And dozens of other websites picked it up. Within twenty-four hours, I went from being a semi-anonymous drone to the pedo king of America. Debates were raging about me on social media.

Morgan's piece not only raised the specter of my marrying a naïve high school girl barely old enough to vote, but also dredged up her suspicious death after we separated, as memorialized in my novella *Torment*. It didn't help matters that Marci's image was soon all over the Internet, and even when she was dressed conservatively, she couldn't help but look eminently fuckable. And very young. "The girl with the movie star face and the porn star body," as I described her in *Freeze Out* during our rapprochement.

He married the girl, didn't he? That was the gist of my defenders' arguments. Which represented about ten percent of the social media posts.

She was in high school, and he had daughters older than her. Eww. This was the seemingly moral majority's point of view.

I had to disable comments on my own social media pages and on the website that Rachel had helped set up for me, including turning off the email option on the site. But that did not prevent me from seeing what was out there. I became a cause celeb for every woke person in the universe. They all hated me. A meme of me and Marci erupted all over the Internet with the caption "Sex Offender", Marci dressed in a schoolgirl outfit to punctuate its message.

I thought Rachel would comfort and console me as I was excoriated across the world. I was wrong. "You made your bed, Phil, now you've got to lie in it." Maybe it was because she was somehow jealous of the young and beautiful, yet dead Marci, I don't know.

Jessica and Anna were mildly supportive. They also said *eww* when they first met my fiancée, but they became friends with Marci, and the three of them would typically join forces to mock me and my lameness, which was cute. But they both now also reminded me I had made my bed and had to lie in it, an expression that came out of the woodwork only to appear in articles written about me all over the fucking place. My best friend Dan just texted me to *"ray row"*. That adorable psychopath.

I texted my recent Manhattan tryst partner Mary Emerick to get her take on all this as a journalist, but my note went from blue to the dreaded green on my iPhone, meaning she had blocked me.

Young people almost unanimously thought I was a creep. Women almost unanimously thought I was a sexual deviant. Most of my defenders were older men with a "good for him, I wish I had hot young tail like that" vibe to their comments. In other words, perverts defended me.

As I have said in my previous narratives, I loved Marci Downes-Allman despite, not because of her youth. We simply connected emotionally, intellectually, and okay, eventually physically; the latter did not occur until our wedding night, however. I helped to rescue her from a really bad situation, as described in my great *Lolita*-esque *Young Blood*. I wanted to go on TV and explain all this on 60 Minutes or something, but Rachel and Bryce Douglas would not allow it.

"There is no such thing as bad publicity, Phil," she said, echoing common thinking. "Your book will likely explode over the next few weeks. The best course right now is to lay low. Bryce's PR team has canceled all of your upcoming interviews. We do not want to add gasoline to this firestorm. Let it burn out on its own."

So. For the next several weeks, I hid away in my apartment. Karma, I guess, for holding Rachel hostage in Uncle Jon's cabin. I called in a couple of favors from Philly PD to sweep away the media trash that waited for me outside of my building's exit. I ordered in food and essentials. Rachel, of course, avoided visiting, not to muddy her good name and reputation. Bryce put out a statement:

Bryce Douglas stands by Phil Allman's new release The Last Shot, *as well as his other novels, which are worthy works of fiction. Mr. Allman's personal life, however, is something for which he alone will have to answer.*

The operative word being *alone*. I became a Woody Allenesque figure, decried by most and defended by a few (mostly perverts).

Meanwhile, *The Last Shot* became a New York Times bestseller, reaching number three on the fiction charts. An amazing accomplishment for a heretofore barely known author. I was not allowed to address the media or even post anything online. Which was good because my natural go-to switch is to become defiant and defensive.

I even made it into a Jimmy Fallon monologue. *"What do you get when you cross a middle-aged writer and a sexy teenage girl? A New York Times bestseller."* (Forced audience laughter) *"Have you heard about this guy..."*

I never said that Jimmy Fallon was funny.

My nine other novels emerged ghostlike from the graves of self-publishing, and all made the Top Fifty bestseller list within that first month. Rachel told me my books were selling well across age and demographic lines; most, she said, read me to reinforce their opinions of me, whether perv or romantic hero. And there was plenty of ammunition in my ten novels to substantiate either position. My nasty divorce from my first wife Cheryl as told in *And I Love Her*. My subsequent marriage to Marci. Other dalliances that made most cringe in the light of recent events.

Other celebrities emerged from such controversies, albeit a bit tainted in the public's eye. Most of them let things simmer down and waited for the public outrage to move on.

And that is exactly what I did.

The buzz died down. But the reading public's curiosity was not satiated. All nine of my previous novels continued to sell well, with my three "Marci" novels (*Young Blood, Freeze Out,* and *Torment*) hitting the New York Times Top Twenty. It was like Elvis's records in the '50s or Beatles' records in the '60s.

And sure enough, this fueled even more interest in Hollywood than had been generated before. But, according to Rachel, most proposed scripts no longer depicted Phil Allman as a tough guy loner, but as a predatory creep. Bryce Douglas had some, but limited control over what, if any, movies were eventually made, but we finally got a balanced treatment offered by two of L.A.'s better screenwriters and one of its more revered directors (not an A-lister, but a solid B), and deals were made, contracts were signed, hands were shaken, and champagne toasts were made.

Phil Allman was coming to a theater near you. Or, more likely, to Netflix or another streaming service in your home. But still, a thrill. Casting calls were made. The director and producers were looking for an actor who could play a tough, mostly honorable, but troubled man. They tossed a few names around, but the filmmakers decided to look at a little-known veteran actor who could pull it off. Some of the bigger Hollywood names carried their own toxic baggage that could turn off many people. At least, that's what I was told.

Lots of actresses were mentioned to play Rachel, including one of my favorites, Marisa Tomei, but it was likely that we would have to settle for someone less well-known under the circumstances. And with this new wrinkle, someone would have to play Marci, and Hollywood had no shortage of smoking hot young actresses who would have done anything (at least in the pre-Harvey Weinstein days) to get the part.

I'm kind of a movie buff, and all of this was wildly

thrilling, even though my life, including some of its more sordid aspects, would be splashed across the screen. Neither Bryce Douglas nor Rachel, and certainly not I had any input into the casting of the movie, nor the direction that it would take now that all of the papers were signed. The control I possessed in writing my novels was gone; shit was going to get portrayed without my applied written consent. Despite that, and the controversy swirling around me, ya boy was summoned to the West Coast by the movie's producers.

That's right, kids. Phil Allman was going to Hollywood.

Chapter 14

I was the only one invited and paid for to go out to L.A. Rachel could have gone on her own dime, but she had to work. She told me to enjoy myself, "but not too much".

If the ends justify the means, then you could say that kidnapping Rachel Arison, who was more or less a stranger at the time, was worth it. I was a bestselling author. I was going out to fucking Hollywood to "take a meeting" with two producer bigwigs, the screenwriters, and the director to offer my input. I would get a screen credit as a Technical Advisor just like Colonel Tom Parker and everything!

It was September by then, and I flew out on Labor Day. I hate early mornings, so I got a direct flight out of Philly at around eleven. I don't fly frequently, and I'm a nervous flyer when I do, so I brought along a book that I had already read and liked. *Lolita*. A little on the nose, but it was good. Not as good as *Young Blood* in my not-so-humble opinion, but good just the same. I know saying that is blasphemous and arrogant, but I encourage you to read both books and you tell me. Which is the better and more believable story?

They told me to pack for a week and only get a one-way ticket, for which I was reimbursed, just in case I had to stay on longer. They put me up in a two-star hotel right on the famous Sunset Boulevard, though not on the famous Sunset Strip. It was within walking distance to Dodger Stadium, however, and I aimed to take advantage of a home game that week. The hotel was in a dicey neighborhood, and a little run down, but so was my apartment building, so it was more than fine by me.

My first impressions of Southern California were of how the mountains seemed like they were scenically placed in the background as in a movie, and how the legends of terrible L.A. traffic were true.

Because of the time change, my late morning flight arrived in mid-afternoon. I was told that it was okay to rent a (small to midsize) car and put all my meals (use discretion though, Phil) on my expense voucher for the production company.

My first meeting wasn't until Wednesday, so I spent a little time meandering around. I went to a Dodgers game that Monday night and was shocked by how well-behaved the crowd was despite losing the game 9-2. Not exactly like a Phillies game at The Bank.

On Tuesday morning, after my "Continental" breakfast (soggy packaged bagels and weak coffee), I drove over to the Getty Museum (good art, incredible views from up in the Hollywood Hills!), then on the way back to the hotel, I found a place to park off of Hollywood Boulevard. I walked on top of the famous stars that represented famous stars. I found the Elvis one and became a little misty; the poor, uneducated boy from Memphis became a bonified movie star. I don't drink much, and have eschewed drugs my whole life, but I stopped into a legal pot shop, and out of curiosity, bought a four-pack of THC-soaked gummies (no matches, no smell), and figured I'd see what the fuss was about before I went to bed that night since I have sleep issues especially when I'm away from home.

I stopped at an outdoor stand a few blocks away from the hotel and got two chicken burritos (mmm!) for less than twenty bucks, and they were the best and juiciest I had ever eaten in my life. My night vision has deteriorated somewhat with age, and I didn't want to schlep around in the chaotic L.A. traffic by eating dinner out, anyway. Plus, the social anxiety thing of dining alone.

Unlike most other novels written in the last twenty years, my books have nary a mention of drugs because they haven't been a part of my life. But the gummies were burning a hole in my pocket. I'm a big guy, so I figured that I would have to take all four to have any effect. And after a half-hour, I was cursing myself for not buying more because I couldn't feel a thing.

However, after an hour, I was having trouble breathing, my heart was pounding, and as I lay in bed, I watched myself from the ceiling, at least metaphorically. I sincerely thought I was going to die. The man on the bed wanted to reach for the phone and call 9-1-1 because I figured I was going to go out like John Belushi or something. But the other me hanging from the ceiling told bed me to relax, that I was going to be fine, and that I didn't want to end up in an L.A. emergency room all night for eating a few gummies; ceiling me also reminded bed me that my shitty healthcare plan had a five-thousand-dollar deductible. I didn't want to piss away my recent good fortune for a bogus death scare. Ceiling me prevailed, and I simply rolled over and went to sleep at eight that night and woke up to the clock radio alarm the next morning at eight. I was still a bit lightheaded, but I was down from my paranoid high.

The experience was surreal; my writing lacks certain surrealism, which I like in others' books, but I wasn't going back to Gummyworld any time soon to further notate the experience.

The meeting was set for nine that Wednesday morning, but two things caused me to arrive almost an hour late. The first was the L.A. traffic, which cannot be overstated. The second was the meeting was at one of the producers' houses way up in the hills, and the combination of my post-gummy high and my hazy vision on the twisting, turning Hollywood Hills roads had me turtling toward my destination at a snail's pace.

But this was Hollywood, and the five men (two producers, two screenwriters, and the director), all tanned, trim, about forty, and very Semitic (some stereotypes are true) welcomed me with hugs. They were understanding that I had underestimated SoCal traffic and joked about my recent media coverage. "Best thing that could have happened to you," was the sentiment. "Out here, you just want them (the ticket-buying public) to know your name. Mission accomplished."

The house wasn't one of the mansions that Raymond Chandler wrote about or anything like the one in *Sunset Boulevard.* It was just a nice ranch-style house, one of about ten on the block, and it was not intimidating. Inside, it was tasteful, with hardwood floors, plenty of sunlight shining through the windows, which gave a magnificent view of the mountains, and the furniture was nice. I don't know anything about furniture, and I don't care to look it up, so "nice" will have to suffice. All five men, as I soon discovered, were surprisingly happily married, and even though this was LaLaLand, I didn't expect any wild orgies or anything on this trip.

When I thought about replying to the assertion that all that matters is that the public knows your name, I was going to suggest that it knew Jeffrey Dahmer's name too, but I didn't want to kill the collegial vibe. We went through the writers' script page by page ("only a first draft, Phil. We want your input, that's why you're here"), and by God, they really did accept most of my ideas and revisions ("You're the real-life Philly detective, Phil, not us. We're going for realism here"). It was one of the more gratifying days of my life, bouncing ideas off of these very smart, successful men. Some novelists go to Hollywood and lambast the executives who bastardize their books. Not this boy. They knew what they were doing, and how to make the gist and the grist of my Phil Allman novels presentable in a hundred-minute movie. "Things have to happen fast on film, Phil. Action action action is what keeps the audience involved."

We only made it through about a quarter of the script that first day. They had decided to condense the first eight novels into that first quarter ("the whole scandalous child bride thing"), and then the rest would be devoted to TLS, my abduction of Rachel, and the ensuing events.

"This is fiction, right, Phil?" the writer asked.

I just shrugged, and they all laughed and laughed. "This crazy guy marries a teenage sexpot and kidnaps a publishing executive. What an imagination!" Ya boy laughed along, and we became fast friends. My usual social anxiety dissipated quickly (an after-effect of the gummies?), and we were like The Six Musketeers. "We're going for a popular, audience-friendly movie here, Phil. But that doesn't mean we can't make it an Oscar-worthy, popular movie. Like a funnier Chinatown." This was Producer One. Number two was mostly Silent Bob, but he took copious notes, and I got the impression that behind the scenes, he was the primary decision-maker.

We had lunch brought in (no alcohol or drugs, unlike the stereotype), just sandwiches and iced tea. At four, we were spinning our wheels creatively, and Producer One suggested we go to one of L.A.'s famous eateries for dinner.

At that early hour, we were seated immediately. "They know us," Producer Two said. I could not help stargazing. At least half of the people in the place were recognizable from television and movies, though I only knew a few of their names. It was exciting, I don't mind saying it.

We sat and ordered soft drinks. "We're all old married men, Phil. If you want a libation or three, please get it," one of the writers said. "Novelists have a reputation, probably well-deserved for drinking in mass quantities."

"Coneheads! Nice," the other writer said.

"Nah, I'm old too," I said. "I'm not a teetotaler, but I don't need to drink. Plus, I have to drive back to the hotel, so this is better, but thanks."

We ordered our fancy schmancy dinners, talked about sports, politics, and of course, movies. These guys might be very successful and wealthy, but they were remarkably down to earth, and could not have been nicer. None of the "L.A. attitude" I was expecting.

"Boy, that journalist really did a number on you, Phil. It seems to have blown over, but that could not have been fun for you," the director said.

"I'm not used to being in the spotlight like many of the people you guys work with. It was difficult, but I live kind of a sheltered life to begin with, so isolating myself in my apartment for a couple of weeks wasn't such a big deal."

The five amigos expressed their empathy and admiration for my resolve. They had no reason to kiss my ass at this point, I just think they were genuinely nice men.

A handful of B-level actors and actresses stopped by the table to pay my new friends their regards, and they introduced me as a "great author whose books were going to make some great *movies*." Plural. Well, we'll see, I guess. The conversation never got stale or stagnant, and we were at the restaurant for almost three hours when Producer One looked at his phone and said, "Hey, Phil, that journalist who gave you that great spread in the New Yorker (that's the magazine and hotel name that I alluded to earlier; puzzle solved) died. Fell off her balcony, of all things. Shame. Her piece is what turned me onto your books. Really sad. How was she when you met her?"

After the free-flowing conversation for several hours, my dumbfounded silence caused them all to stare at me, waiting for an answer. I finally said, "She was very nice. Like you said, it's tragic."

At which point, Producer Two waved to the waitress and mimed writing a checkmark for her. "I'm sorry to end our nice evening on such a sour note, Phil.

If you want to take tomorrow off, it's okay." The other guys echoed that generous sentiment.

"No, I'll be fine, but thanks. It's just a bit shocking. Mary Emerick could not have been kinder to me. Kind of like you guys. I was expecting a snotty, snobby attitude from all of you, but it didn't happen." We man-hugged and expressed some more mutual admiration. One of the producers paid the check, and then plans were made to meet back at the house the next morning at ten.

"Give you a chance to sleep in a little, Phil," Producer Two said.

We drove back to the house, and I got in the rental car and meandered to the hotel. It wasn't dark yet, and traffic wasn't too awful in the early evening hour. During the drive, I thought one thing, probably what you are thinking right now.

People don't fall off balconies. Unless they're high or drunk. Or unless they're pushed.

Chapter 15

We finished our script revisions by Thursday, and the guys told me to take the next few days on their dime, and I did. I spent a day at Venice Beach (funky!), Santa Monica Beach (peaceful!), and another driving in the rain up the Pacific Coast Highway to Malibu (scenic!), and various other sundry excursions around the city. I won't go into detail, except to say I found the people in Southern California surprisingly nice and down to earth. I took a late morning flight back that Sunday, and was able to get back home not too late, despite the time difference.

I had no clue what to do about Rachel. Should I confront her about Mary Emerick and see what she had to say? Was the journalist murdered because of some jealousy of Rachel's, which, while horrible, was flattering, I have to admit. Or should I let it go and see if she brought the subject up? Obviously, the death of the most famous journalist in the book industry, not to mention one with whom I recently met, was not something Rachel could be unaware of.

Of course, it could all be a weird coincidence. Maybe Mary really did fall off her balcony after perhaps taking a drink too many. Suicide could not be ruled out; we never know what someone is going through. The NYPD seemed content to deem it an accident, and they weren't slouches.

I could do my due diligence and have Dan Lee track Rachel's movements over the past week while I was in Los Angeles. Did she go up to New York? Was she in Mary's zip code? Or her building? Dan could discover these things. But like one of my favorite Elvis songs, *I Really Don't Want To Know*. Look for it, his vocal is awesome.

Ignorance is bliss, I believe it. I was not going to turn my benefactor and hostage into the authorities anyway, so what would be the point? I had enough controversy still swirling around me (though it had died down) without adding my kidnapping escapade to the swirl.

I was a bestselling, world-famous writer. With at least one movie based on my writing in the works by a formidable Hollywood team (the B Team, but still). Maybe more movies down the line. Phil Allman could be the new Mike Hammer. Or dare I say Philip Marlowe?

I could have gone to any book fair in the country and gotten hot author groupies. Two at a time, like on Pornhub (from what I have been told, of course). The public's venom had turned to other targets. "Okay, he went after a young girl. But he *married* her, didn't he?" This was now the prevailing, lingering sentiment. It's not like she was my de facto stepdaughter. My daughters had put out a public statement reaffirming that I was a good father and a great husband to Marci (I would have preferred "great" for both), and Bryce's Public Relations people did a good job in tamping down the hate and building public support.

I was riding high, living the dream, making bank, and all the rest. So, my pseudo-girlfriend might be a mass murderer. You can't have everything, am I right?

I was settling back into my apartment, my old life, except with a ton of money in the bank and a ton more to come. There was no need to write now. I had ten books total in the can, and I thought that I would take a break from everything. Football season was about to start again, with the baseball playoffs and the basketball season not far behind. I could finally become a man of leisure.

As I was thinking these peaceful thoughts while unpacking that Monday afternoon, I heard someone buzz, wanting access to my apartment. I pressed the speaker, and it was a Western Union guy, of all people. I was being delivered a real-life telegram, the first in my life, if you don't count Psycho Dan's silly text.

I went downstairs, signed for it, and waited until I was back in my apartment to read it. This could not be good news. Nobody sends good news via telegram, or at least that is what I had heard over the years. This one held to form.

Mr. Allman, we regret to inform you that Rachel Arison took her own life yesterday. This will not reach the media until tomorrow. I know that you and Rachel became more than publishing advocate and author, and I deliver this news with great sadness. Bryce Douglas remains committed to you and your work, and if you need anything from us, or me personally, please call me on my personal cell. As funeral arrangements become available, I will get them to you immediately. We at Bryce Douglas are heartbroken, and I suspect you will be as well.

-Raymond Orenstein, Bryce Douglas President and CEO

Chapter 16

There was a period of grief that surprised me in its intensity. I had obviously been through a lot with Rachel, and had grown quite fond of her. I didn't love her exactly, but she helped to make my dreams come true, and did so out of something close to love. I think that she really believed in me, and I can't say that about many.

I am not an armchair psychiatrist, and I did not know if Rachel was confessing to anything by killing herself. I am an investigator, and I could investigate it, but I chose not to, at least for the moment. It did not matter. If Rachel was involved in the deaths of Alyssa, Andrea, and Mary, I suppose you could say those women attained justice, finally, with Rachel's death. If she was not involved, then somebody else would have to find that out. Officially, all three deaths were unexplained; in the cases of Andrea and Mary, they were deemed accidents. And of course, Alyssa's murder was still unsolved. What good would it do anyone or anything to dredge all that up at this point?

Nor did I look into Rachel's death. I took it as gospel that it was suicide. I subsequently learned that there was no note, and the cause of death was asphyxiation as the result of an abundance of barbiturates and alcohol in her system. The usual method of women who off themselves, to put it

Britishly.

Jessica and Anna were sympathetic, but they couldn't understand why I was so broken up about Rachel's death. I had never let them know that we were "dating", nor had I shared the tidbit about kidnapping her to get my book deal. Hey, do you think they told me every intimate detail of their lives? Any parent who thinks their kids tell all is an idiot.

—She was the lady at the publishing company, right?— Anna asked when I texted her the horrible news after I received the telegram. —It is sad. Are you going to the funeral?— she texted back.

—I don't know.— And I didn't. As her protégé, it would make sense to show up. But I didn't own a black suit and hated funerals because they reminded me too much of my own mortality. Probably though.

Jessica too expressed her condolences but did not get why I was so sad. "Did you date her, Daddy?" She is a perceptive girl, taking after her mother.

"Not really. We became friends and went out a couple of times socially. But mostly to talk about the book." And that was that.

Dan knew more than the girls, but he knew better than to bother me at that moment.

—*Seem rikecrassyrady*— was all the psychopath texted me.

Because curiosity was killing this cat, I sent him a brief reply, asking for a report regarding geographic proximities to the deaths of Alyssa, Andrea, Mary, and even Rachel, to scratch an itch that I suppose never dies in an investigator until he or she dies.

I ended up going to the funeral that Wednesday. It was a lovely day for a lovely woman, temps in the seventies, sunny, light breeze. It was an outdoor service at a Jewish cemetery right off of Roosevelt Boulevard, just north of Philly in a town called Trevose. It was a small, obviously somber gathering. It didn't look like her New York colleagues showed up, just about a dozen people who were extended family members. The service was brief, and when somebody shoveled a heap of dirt onto the coffin before they lowered it into the ground, I shed a tear. Yes, I did.

Oh, and my buddy Stanley Kret was there. Surprisingly. Classy move, I admit. He tried extremely hard not to look at me, but since there were so few attendees, he could not avoid my glare. He was still out on bail on his illegal porn arrest, so who knew how many more free days he would have?

Rachel's sister Karen gave a thirty-second eulogy; "brilliant, driven, loyal" were the adjectives she used to describe Rachel, sounding more like good qualities for a job applicant than a dead sibling who killed herself, but it was adequate, and I suppose appropriate. I was invited to come over to the sister's house to "sit shiva" and nosh on some good, free food, but I declined. I thought about my new fancy schmancy furniture at home, realizing Rachel Arison bought it for me. And filled my bank account to the point where I'd never have to work again if I didn't want to.

I checked my phone and saw a text from the Hollywood director, updating me on how things were going as far as casting, and expressing his condolences about my friend and publisher.

Soon, my little psychobabble stories would be on the silver screen. They already dominated the brick-and-mortar and online bookshelves. All because a smart, overachieving lady with whom I had gone to high school (but to whom I had never spoken then) made it all possible after a selfish, narcissistic asshole kidnapped her and made her do it.

I should have felt more guilty than I did, but being a narcissistic asshole, I still felt like I deserved my ill-gotten fame and fortune. Ain't that a kick in the head, to quote Mr. Sinatra?

I had one last rose of gratitude to toss to Rachel Arison. I could not let the lowering of the coffin kill that off.

****

I was wildly grief-stricken and wildly angry as I drove away from the cemetery. There was no procession of limos with headlights on; a few vehicles headed to Rachel's sister's home for shiva. Kret probably knew he would not exactly be welcomed, so give him kudos for self-awareness. He drove toward the Pennsylvania Turnpike entrance less than a mile away, which would have led him to the New Jersey Turnpike, and then to his apartment in Chelsea. Dan had already texted me that it was indeed Kret's own vehicle, a white Honda sedan, which surprised me given that he lived in Manhattan, and was likely paying thousands of dollars a year just to park it. We all have our creature comforts.

I could not allow him access to get on the turnpike, of course. As he stopped at the light that would have put him on Roosevelt Boulevard, I drove up behind him, honked twice, and motioned for him to turn off into the parking lot of a convenience store to our right. He did so, which surprised me.

Kret parked, and I got out of my car, leaving the motor running, and approached him on the driver's side. He rolled his window down, and I opened my suit jacket to show him the gun that was in my jacket pocket and told him to get into my car. Again, surprisingly, he did so.

We said nothing once we drove away from the convenience store lot. Maybe Kret carried around the weight of guilt besides his obese weight. I don't know. And I don't care.

Dan's reports, which he had texted me an hour before the funeral began, showed that only one person was in the same zip codes as Alyssa, Andrea, Mary, and Rachel at the times of their deaths. Thank God it wasn't Rachel, though I thought it probably was. And maybe, just maybe, with his soon-to-be trial and sure-thing conviction for possession of child porn, he just didn't want to live anymore.

I drove us to a nearby park that was adjacent to the famous Delaware River. I motioned for Kret to exit the car, which he did. Again, not a word, not a twitch, not a complaint.

My radar for understanding people and reading the truth had been going awry for some time. Obviously, I was wrong about Kret's innocence when I throttled him in his apartment. I really believed him and had actually felt sorry for him.

We were at the river's edge, at a spot that I had predetermined was out of sight from vehicular and pedestrian traffic.

I've complained about the state of mystery novels a lot in this narrative. The worst is when the mass murderer goes on for twenty pages at the end explaining his motives and tactics to the hero cop/P.I./good Samaritan citizen/whomever. There was none of that with Kret, and there will be none of that here. He accepted his fate with more manliness (if that's not a banned politically incorrect word) than I would have expected.

Kret was bulky more than heavy when I weighed his suit down with actual small weights that I had lying around my apartment. I pushed him into the river after firing one bullet into his forehead. I felt no guilt; he was a predator, an abuser, and a murderer of four innocent women.

I've mentioned Woody Allen in this narrative. He has to live with his transgressions, whether those of moral failing (sleeping with his de facto stepdaughter), or his alleged criminal behavior (molesting his own young daughter). None of that takes away from his work, as he wrote and directed some of the greatest and funniest movies of the '70s and '80s. The best of which, *Crimes and Misdemeanors,* is about how people are often rewarded for bad behavior and punished for good.

Meaning there is no karma, no justice, and in the end, no God.

I hate feeling that way, but the cynical detective, writer, and Philadelphian that I am, I believed it. And lived it.

I was rewarded with a massive book publishing contract and subsequent movie deal for kidnapping Rachel Arison. I was renumerated with incredible sales in large part for controversially marrying the sexy, vulnerable, teenaged Marci Downes, and sleeping with the famous literary tastemaker Mary Emerick. I have not and will not be punished for taking the law into my own hands and murdering Stanley Kret. This is how life actually works.

I don't know if there will be another Phil Allman novel. I'm rich, famous, and not too old yet to enjoy the spoils that come with wealth and fame. As I intimated at the beginning of this book, morality is dead.

And I'm going to have myself a time. Before the fourth quarter is over.

A word about the author...

Brett Wallach was born and raised in a working-class household and neighborhood in Philadelphia, didn't begin reading fiction for pleasure until he was in his late twenties, and did not start writing it until he was about forty. Brett graduated from Penn State, has had a long, checkered career in Corporate Sales, and he has two daughters in their twenties. Brett writes noir fiction because "I think that most people are neither all good nor bad, and most of us might do bad and/or good things in pursuit of love, money, notoriety, and sex." Brett's novels are funny, but they are definitely edgy and even controversial, and not meant for every reader. *The Last Shot* is his ninth novel in the Phil Allman, P.I. series, and his tenth overall. He currently lives in suburban Philadelphia.

Thank you for purchasing
this publication of The Wild Rose Press, Inc.

For questions or more information
contact us at
info@thewildrosepress.com.

The Wild Rose Press, Inc.
www.thewildrosepress.com